Falling Backwards

Falling
Backwards

JAMES QUINN

[Lacuna]
2013

All enquiries to the publisher: general@lacunapublishing.com

Published in 2013 by Lacuna
http://www.lacunapublishing.com

Lacuna is an imprint of Golden Orb Creative
PO Box 185, Westgate NSW 2048, Australia
http://www.goldenorbcreative.com

Cover design by Golden Orb Creative
Text layout by Golden Orb Creative
Typeset in 10.5/12.6 pt Minion Pro.

National Library of Australia Cataloguing-in-Publication entry

Quinn, James, author.

Falling backwards / James Quinn.

ISBN 9781922198044 (paperback)

ISBN 9781922198051 (eBook)

A823.4

Contents

Autumn

IT WAS ABOUT a year ago, when I wasn't worth much of anything at all. I was wearing a cheap black suit, which was something that they used to make me do back then. Anything else would have invited mean-spirited remarks at the lamington drives and on bingo nights. The suit was cheap and I had no say in the matter. Too flashy and it would have undone all the lying and cups of milky tea. From where I was sitting I could hear the fridge burring in the kitchen and a magpie warbling in the frangipani outside. It was late in the evening and I could smell the garden cooling with the dew. I sat quietly in my lounge room in a fat old armchair, sharing the space uncomfortably with Donald and Mary. Together the three of us inhaled and exhaled away an awkward moment. Donald and Mary were regulars at my marriage counselling sessions and the topic for the evening was a difficult one.

Donald, Mary and I formed a lopsided triangle around a scuffed timber coffee table in the lounge room of my house. There was a writing desk behind me and behind that a wall of books. A big red Bible was wedged between a number of texts on the human condition. I glanced across at Mary. She sat very erect, her knees pressed together femininely, and she occasionally brushed a few strands of hair out of her eyes with her right hand and over her ear. I registered the tension in her posture and in her elegant spine curving out to her bottom. Donald leant forward in his chair anxiously, his hands clasped between his knees and head bowed. The sessions were very hard on Donald. He found it difficult to express his feelings and I used to draw every revelation and admission out of him slowly and painfully. Poor Donald. I feel sorry for him even now. I really do.

The topic for the evening was intimacy. It was really the same subject every week with those two. Specifically, the subject was the *lack* of intimacy between Donald and Mary. No sex for months and when it happened, he was premature. I still wonder why they even bothered. I didn't need qualifications to know that Donald and Mary's marriage was going down the toilet. Mary sat opposite me quietly as I tentatively drew a series of humiliations out of the man that she once loved more than words can express (her words, not mine). Donald spoke softly. Poor bastard. I recall going easy on him because he really didn't deserve all this. And Mary? She didn't look especially uncomfortable. If anything, I'd say she may even have been enjoying it. I looked in her direction and saw smugness, which didn't suit her.

To tell the truth, I was tired. It had been a long day coming at the end of a long week. I had been woken at 4.30 that morning by another person who had needed to talk. And so we had talked. I guess that was my job back then. Talking. Actually, not talking, listening. I never used to say much at all and when I did, no-one really listened. But that's okay. I got used to it. I made a living keeping a lid on it. It wearied me some days, and it was wearying me that day and so only distantly I heard Donald telling us that Mary's body didn't do it for him any more. He couldn't say when it started and he couldn't say why. Mary shifted angrily in her chair, clearly hurt, so Donald stopped talking and winced. He knew he had stung her, someone he still loved, and anticipated a sharp-tongued rebuke, but Mary stayed silent. Fearing that she might cry I stepped in, distracted her with a question, and then started wrapping things up. Poor Donald. Poor Mary. I was so tired and it was all so sad.

I recall Donald and me getting to our feet and the two of us shuffling towards the door. He relaxed a little as his escape approached. It was always a relief for him when he left my company, like most of the men I knew back then, which was another thing that I had learned to grow used to. Mary stayed seated in the other room. We had scheduled some follow-up one-on-one therapy, so Donald and I left the office and entered what we called 'the lobby'. It was really just the sun room of the house that they gave me. We shook hands at the front door and then shared some more foot-shuffling. Donald looked incredibly grateful. I think he probably wanted to hug me. I told him that I knew how hard it was for him. I remember him agreeing and him telling me how difficult it can be to forget that I was also his pastor, the preacher at his church. I reminded him that I was a qualified marriage counsellor too and he nodded, and assured me that he understood. He shrugged then paused and smiled weakly. As he left I closed the door gently behind him and sighed. Such a long day. So tired. So weary.

I returned to the office. Mary had her back to me. She was bending over my desk with her skirt hitched up over her hips and I could see that she was wearing no underpants. Post-session sex was always the sexiest. Her gorgeous round bottom beckoned. She looked back over her shoulder and said softly, 'Can you do it from behind tonight?' I walked across the room to her. Mary remained bent forward with her bum sticking out and I stood behind her and closed my eyes as she pressed backwards into my groin. She was soft and womanly. Her hair, her neck, her shoulders were fragrant, a potent and *female* smell. I knelt down and pressed my cheek against her smooth round bottom. She rested her hands on her knees, shifting her feet a little further apart for me. She was so lovely and I was so tired. I closed my eyes and kissed her soft inner thighs thinking, why should I resist this and why should I feel shame? She had a warm kind heart. She loved me in her way. 'Yes,' I said, rising to my feet again and unbuckling my belt, 'That sounds like a wonderful idea.'

*   *   *

Back then I would have said, 'And who could blame me?' And who could? That week had started with the phone ringing at 2am and me rolling groggily out of sleep to answer it in the darkness. An early morning phone call was always bad news and sure enough thirty minutes later I was on the front steps of a dingy terrace house in Paddington. As I walked in the door a policeman came out of the bedroom and moved down the hall, hunching his shoulders against the narrow space. It was Jamie, a Kings Cross veteran. 'Simon!' he said, looking a little relieved. 'Thanks for coming, mate. We have a bit of a situation.' He led me back into the bedroom where a woman lay on the floor beside the bed. She was curled onto her side and blood had dribbled from her nose, leaving a small dark puddle on the floorboards beside her nostril. Her eye was swollen and her forehead grazed. She was barely conscious, beaten senseless and high on drugs. Another copper stood by the window looking out onto the empty night-time street. He'd have been bored if he hadn't been so disgusted. Jamie and I moved towards the girl and together we tried to turn her over. The other copper made no move to help so the two of us struggled with her ragdoll body and together we lifted her up and onto the bed. The woman resented us all the way, mumbling incoherently, squirming weakly to break our hold. She was dressed in tight jeans and a grubby t-shirt. Her feet were dirty and bare, the toenails painted blue, the nail polish peeling. Jamie told the other policeman to go into the kitchen and make some tea and when he had slouched out of the room Jamie filled me in.

The woman was a hooker, and a punter had done the dirty on her. Bashed her, raped her, stolen the little money she had in her purse and walked out leaving her half-conscious on the floor. A neighbour had heard the fuss and had called the police. The victim, in a lucid moment, had refused to go to the hospital. She had insisted on no ambulances. Jamie had had a hard time just keeping her in the bed. Stoned out of her mind, she kept rolling onto the floor and curling into the foetal position. I suggested he take her to the lock-up but Jamie shook his head in the negative. 'We have a new bloke down there who wouldn't see it our way. He'd insist on charging her.' I looked at her bloodied face. 'What with, for Christ's sake?' I asked angrily. Jamie raised his eyebrows and gestured towards the dresser beside the bed. A couple of little plastic bags sat on the top, a residue of clear crystal meth still visible inside. A little laugh. 'Take your pick,' he said. 'Drugs, prostitution, you name it. Look, mate. I can't stick around here all night and I'm worried she'll overdo the drugs if we leave her alone.' He didn't finish the sentence. I knew what he was asking. I told him I'd stay with her till she started coming out of it and he thanked me. 'I don't want a stiff on my watch,' he half-joked. Jamie was a good guy. He could have just left her and plenty of blokes would have.

Jamie and the other copper walked out and I was left with a cup of hot sweet tea and a half-conscious prostitute. She was sleeping on her side on the bed, her back to me. I tried to rouse her, offer her a cuppa. Her instinctual response was anger.

6

She roared at me to get fucked so I just left it alone. She rolled her back to me again and drifted off to sleep, snoring gently. I looked around the room. Bare. Hardly a piece of furniture in it save the old bed and a faded chest of drawers and dresser. No photographs. No art. I stepped into her bathroom. It was filthy. I checked the cabinet. Toothbrush. Toothpaste. Panadol. A small bottle of prescription drugs. A condom packet. I walked down the hall to the tiny kitchen and found myself a chair. I took it back into the bedroom and made myself comfortable beside the window. I took my wallet and mobile phone out of my pockets and put them on the window sill and after a time I drifted off to sleep.

I woke an hour or so later to hear the woman sobbing. The room reeked. She had defecated herself. Gagging, I tried to take her jeans off but she was still half asleep and half drug-fucked, her arms and legs flopping, head lolling, as I dragged first her trousers down her wasted thighs, then her underpants. I left her sprawled on the bed, naked except for her t-shirt, about as sexless as nudity can get, and threw the jeans and knickers into the bathtub, closing the door on the smell. I couldn't bring myself to clean her any more so I drew the sheet up over her naked arse and returned to my seat. Dawn soon. The sky was turning to pale grey. What a life. Hers and mine.

I waited until about 8am and then shook the woman awake. The drugs were wearing off but her face was still a mess. The blood had dried. Her eye was bruised. She looked at me bleary-eyed but, accustomed to finding strange men in her bedroom, she exhibited every emotion except scared. 'Who the fuck are you?' she demanded angrily. I told her. She seemed unimpressed. 'Get me a wet towel,' she ordered so I went to the stinking bathroom and found a towel, ran it under the tap and returned to the bedroom. She was standing by the bed still naked from the waist down. 'What the fuck?' she said, palms up. 'You shat yourself,' I told her. She took the wet towel and wiped her bloodied face, glancing at me as she did so, then she cleaned between her legs as if I were not in the room. She looked alright in spite of the beating so I took up my wallet and phone and told her she should see a doctor. I told her she should take better care of herself, trying not to sound patronising but maybe getting the intonation wrong. 'Get fucked,' she said. There was no point sticking around now so I said a simple good-bye and made my way back down the hallway leaving the woman to her soiled pants, her drugs, and her cheap painted toenails. As I closed the front door behind me I paused to roll the aches out of my shoulders then made my way through a dim morning to the taxi rank. It looked like rain. It was only when the taxi pulled up outside my home and I tried to pay that I found that the hooker had stolen every note in my wallet. It had been one of those nights I guess. Just one of those nights.

*   *   *

The night after my session with Donald and Mary and we were talking about giving it up to God. This time it was prayer group. Tuesdays. 7.30pm kick-off, usually over by 10. We always started with twenty minutes of song – up-tempo religious numbers with a funky rhythm, all played out in my lounge room to the accompaniment of a tambourine (Caroline with the bucked teeth) and an acoustic guitar (Caroline with the armpit hair). I was an understated preacher by all reports. I ran the Tuesday prayer group but I used to try to take a backseat. During the singing, I'd sing along. In spite of everything, I must admit that I quite liked the songs, but when the singing stopped and the time came for me to speak, I found myself doing so less and less enthusiastically. Actually, I did it totally without enthusiasm. They used to misinterpret my reticence as a sober shyness. They were all plain gullible come to think of it but they were nice people I suppose, for the most part. I suppose.

That night, I hadn't prepared. That had been going to happen the previous night but Mary's bottom had put paid to that, so I just sat in front of the room of assembled faithful, groin throbbing gently with the memory of Mary, and spoke to them of generic God-things. He's kind. He's all-seeing. He's just and forgiving. My words were punctuated with ardent muttered amens from the congregation. Not African-American gospel amens. We were all white-bread Australians of the essentially Protestant ilk, with a smattering of recovering abused Catholics in our midst, so we didn't go in for the really big amens. Not on a Tuesday. That was for the youngsters in the Sunday services.

For a preacher I didn't really like talking about God that much but that was all part of the role that I played, and for a few hours every week it wasn't so hard. It was much easier when we were in New Testament territory. I could talk about that stuff all night. I enjoyed encouraging people to do unto others as they would have others do unto them, but they always wanted to steer it back to the Old Testament eventually. They loved it. Gods that smite. They especially liked Gods that smite single mothers and gays. A lot of stones used to get cast in Bible Group, and when I'd say 'Let he who is without sin cast the first stone' they'd seem non-plussed. I loved the New Testament but they'd look at me as if I was a spoilsport, as if to say, there has to be some judging, surely!

That night Donna was keen to speak. Donna was one of the women who *never* missed prayer group. She was middle-aged and plain. She baked scones that were middle-aged and plain. She'd bring the scones to prayer group every week wrapped in grubby tea towels. They were hard little things, like her heart. I ignored her for a few minutes until I knew it was almost killing her, and then I asked her if she had any thoughts she'd like to share. That was what prayer group was really all about for her: a captive audience forced before God to endure her gobshite. She told me that she had the perfect psalm for that night's theme, one that was all about God's immeasurable beauty and strength. She opened her Bible and nominated some psalm. She could have referred us to any of them really. They're all about God's power and how he can really fuck you over if you don't watch out. I suggested that Donna read it aloud for us which she acceded to graciously, a slight nod of her head, looking me in the eye as if to say 'what a good man you are'. She should have seen me going down on Mary the night before. 'Good' was barely scratching the surface.

At about that time I was starting to get introspective about it all. As Donna read the scripture I allowed my mind to wander. 'How the hell did I get here?' I thought to myself. 'I'm thirty-seven years old. I'm neither tall nor short, fat nor thin. Non-descript, I suppose you'd say. A university degree. No car. I'm unmarried. And I live my life surrounded by the delusional!' That was my cross to bear: a congregation of numpties.

Donna read on. The psalm was all about how we must love God or suffer the consequences. 'Praise God,' said a woman's voice from the left. It was Jenny. I knew Jenny well. The year before, her husband had fractured her cheek bone after a night on the turps by hitting her with the bread board. Another 4am telephone call and me driving to her place to break up the fight. What a scene. Her dreadful abused face swollen from the beating and Jenny weeping, her husband slumped on the lounge in his shorts, too drunk to speak but human enough for seething rage. He could have killed me that night. The church had given her a room for three weeks after that and we had given her the bond on a new flat, with money for food, but she had gone back to him. In fact, they're still together now, love-hating each other in a marriage of fear. It was one of our church's proudest achievements. Jenny was listening to Donna's words with her eyes closed and head bowed, concentrating on every syllable. I remember thinking, 'What can she possibly be getting out of all this talk of the God that loves and smites?' But, of course, she got it better than any of us. It was an abusive relationship and we had to suffer through it.

After Tuesday prayer group I was pretty much obliged to speak to them. That was the price I paid for the exquisite nibblies. That, and Donna's scones. Prayer group had as much to do with the competitive baking as it did with God. *More* when Nancy made shortbread. Basically, we'd talk about God for a while then stick our noses in the trough. In cold graves across the Mediterranean, the bodies of ascetic monks would turn in horror. Portly women would demurely squeeze cream buns into pinched little mouths, mouths that 15 minutes earlier had been giving it to Moslems and divorcees and the other children of Satan. And there was the sex of course. Not penis-in-vagina real sex. It was pseudo-sex. Outrageous flirtation. I'd spend the after-prayer-group get-together being stroked and patted and pinched. Arms were put around me. My hand would get held and squeezed. I'd leave the meetings feeling molested. More women engaged in body contact with me on a Tuesday evening than at any other time in my life. And so cleaning up after Tuesday prayer group was like cleaning up after bad sex – sex with a charmless woman, a woman you didn't respect. The crumpled coagulated tissues, the condom and the ooze of semen in it, cooling to the temperature of the floor boards by the bed. It was the same with the cream-smeared saucers and the plastic cups with soggy crumbs in the bottom. You had to pick them up, touch them, dispose of them.

Sister Patti and Sister Pru were helping me with the cleaning up that night, as they always did. They were the two old ladies who looked after the crèche during the week. They were former nuns, drummed out of the profession for unspecified sins, who had found a place for themselves in the Ministry of Christ where the 'Sister' moniker had stuck, although as a rule we didn't go in for that nonsense in our church. Both ladies were bending under their years, thin women with stooped shoulders and narrow hips. They shared a house together and seemed unconcerned about which cardigan they pulled out of the cupboard. Sometimes Pru would wear Patti's favourite, sometimes Patti would wear Pru's. They seemed interchangeable. They had dark veins on the backs of their bony hands and looked like they would snap if you hugged too hard, but when a child fell from the swings at the crèche, Patti's and Pru's arms were always open and enfolding and their cooing kind voices would soothe the sobs away. That night they stayed back late and collected the plastic cups frugally. They would wash them and re-use them to save money. Cold water, they would tell me, because hot water splits the plastic. I think that I must have still been very tired and it must have been showing. I cleaned one side of the room while they worked the other, leaving me in peace. I loved them. Of the entire congregation only they knew when not to speak to me.

We finished the cleaning up in silence then Patti came over to me and rested a hand on my forearm. 'You look like you need a good home-cooked dinner,' she said with a cocked right eyebrow. I accepted her offer and arranged to come round for dinner a couple of nights later. As they left, Pru paused and said, 'Simon, you must rest'. 'Tell that to Mary's bum,' I was tempted to say, but didn't.

* * *

I was usually late in rising on Wednesday mornings. I found that Tuesday praying could really take it out of you, but I always used to be in The Mission by 11am. The Mission was a ground-floor room in a terrace house on Darlinghurst Road in Kings Cross. From the front room I used to have a perfect view of the XXX porn store across the road and the kebab shop next door to it, run by Minh, the Vietnamese drug seller. Walk into the store for a kebab and he would greet you with a cheery 'Salaam'.

The Mission was furnished with a simple second-hand desk and a variety of cheap plastic chairs, none of them matching. There was a bar fridge in one corner containing non-alcoholic drinks and, in an ice-cream container in the vegetable cooler, about fifty clean hypodermic needles. At the front of the room, by the window, there was a rack containing a variety of brochures. They were all about God and Jesus. Gregory, the head of our church, used to make me put them there. Lots of American-produced cartoonish pictures of Jesus. There was Jesus looking very smug, having just turned the water into wine, his self-satisfied expression saying 'get a load of this!' And Jesus going for a stroll on the Sea of Galilee, hitching his skirt a little to avoid getting the hem wet. My favourite was Jesus bricking it in the Garden of Gethsemane in the hours before his arrest. Who paints these pictures? They were, I'm afraid, wasted on my clientele whose first instinct would more likely have been to offer poor Jesus a head job than pray to him. My clientele, you see, were generally working girls who viewed the world with clinical cynicism. They had seen it all. They had done it all. They had abused their bodies with alcohol and drugs. They had given their bodies to men who had abused them still more. They had little regard for men with kind eyes. They could be very hard ladies, which is not to say bad.

That Wednesday passed quietly. A couple of girls dropped by, asking for clean needles. A couple of coppers doing their rounds dropped in for a chat. They seemed so young. As we chatted, they rearranged the accoutrements of their profession on their giant black belts: handcuffs, revolver, night stick, mace holsters. A reminder that when it all goes horribly wrong they are the ones that clean it up. We compared news, rumours and gossip and they strolled back into the street, waving to a couple of girls working the opposite corner as they went. The girls smiled, waved back, grinned at each other, and returned to toeing the footpath agitatedly as they waited for a punter. Mostly, the world passed them by, ignoring, not caring.

Late in the day Evie dropped by, tossing me a chocolate bar as she walked through the door. Evie had a great smile and a sassy attitude. She'd swing her hips when she walked, not as an affectation but because she was just plain sexy, prostitute or not. She was only in her early twenties and not yet hard. One day I figured she would tell me why she was there doing those things but I didn't need to push it. 'Hey preacher,' she called cheekily. 'Hi Evie,' I replied. 'What brings you down here?' 'Thought I might get a kiss,' she said and we both smiled. I opened the chocolate bar and took a bite, offering Evie a bit, but she turned her nose up at it and watched me chew while we chatted. 'So what's up?' I asked. Evie half thought about it and said, 'Nothing,' as if that disappointed her. 'I'm just off to work and thought I'd stop by and chat to a man who doesn't want to do me for once.' She looked about the room absently then settled a sneaky grin on me like she suddenly remembered it was a challenge. 'You can say *that* again!' 'Naughty preacher,' Evie said with a wave of her finger. 'If that's the best you can do, I'm off.' She stood up to leave, taking mock offence, but paused to look at me, hands on hips. 'Oh come on,' she complained. 'Just one widdle kiss.' She puckered for me in mock readiness but I waved her away. 'Fine, I had things to do anyway.' She turned haughtily and walked out laughing, swinging her hips extravagantly for my benefit. 'Stop looking, ya perv,' she called over her shoulder as she disappeared out the door, leaving me suddenly very much alone. Just me and a grubby world outside the window. I'd had six years of it by then and after six years I could claim to be something of an expert on the subject of street prostitution. Let me tell you, it's no picnic.

At the end of the day I closed the front door on The Mission, pulled down the metal security screen and locked it tight. I headed home to my empty house, buying some Thai takeaway on the way. Inside my house it was silent and cold. Mainly, it was empty. It would have saddened some people, I suppose. I slopped the noodles into a bowl and flicked on the telly, then slumped on the lounge in front of it. It was late evening. Crickets were chirping away any lingering memories of summer in the little courtyard out the back door. After a day of XXX and policemen and needles and prostitutes I found myself watching one of those earnest British fly-on-the-wall documentaries set in a sleety north England town. That was all I needed after a day in the Cross. A documentary about prostitution! But I couldn't stop myself watching. They were following some poor girl from street corner to back seat of cheap car with just a touch too much eagerness, charting every blow job with monotone voiceovers and slightly blurred rhythmic close-ups, on zoom from across bleak streets. They were telling a very worthy story and the message was clear: it is not a victimless crime. But I remember being confounded by something else. It was the interview with the prostitute. She was sitting in some dismal housing scheme building, sucking on a cigarette that had been paid for with some, believe me, hard-earned cash, recounting her experiences of men. She told us that she likes men generally. Then lazily, dazedly, with an air of boredom that reflected the dullness of the walls behind her, she told us what they liked. She sucked on that cigarette again, not looking at the camera, breathing the smoke out as she spoke. Not showy. Not at all showy.

'Some of them like anal,' she ventured with a disinterested half-shrug, but her lips pursed and her eyes squinted as she considered her own words. A thoughtful silence then, 'Some like oral.' More thinking. 'Sixty-nine ... doggy ... plain missionary ...'

She was getting into the swing of it now. 'Some like kinky ... dress ups ... dildos ... Some like to be spanked.' She catalogued the depravities and paused at the end with something of a sigh, a bored sigh not an indignant one. Then she said a remarkable thing. With her eyes cast down and to the side, and evidently having exhausted the list of sexual acts she had been asked to perform, she concluded with the striking observation, almost an afterthought really. 'Um ... they *all* leave their socks on.'

She seemed genuinely offended by that one. Really put out about it. Anal had barely rated a shrug! But, you see, this is at the heart of the transaction. Fat men with humid armpits, kicking off their shoes, and not bothering with the socks.

*   *   *

The following evening Sister Patti and Sister Pru gave me an enormous brandy as the final stage in the consumption of a mammoth baked dinner with all the trimmings. We stood in their lounge room giving their framed photos a once-over while Patti and Pru started on the sherry. A photograph of the two women on the bookcase caught my eye. It must have been decades old. The women were dressed in dated swimsuits and stood arm in arm on a beach somewhere, beaming at the camera. I picked it up and turned with an inquiring raising of the eyebrow. They both looked stunning. Patti fondly took the picture from my hands, Pru moved closer, and we all stood there in our little group gazing at the image. 'We joined the penguins at the same time,' said Patti. 'The same age to the month,' added Pru. 'Yes, two girls from the bush, lonely in the Big Smoke,' said Patti with a nostalgic sigh, and shook her head as if she couldn't really believe it was her. Pru angled the photo so I could get a better view and told me, 'This was taken a week after we packed it in. It was never really for us you see. We really weren't cut out for the Catholic Church.' Patti nodded and finished Pru's train of thought. 'They sneered when we left. I can still see their faces. But we look happy there, don't we.'

I looked at the photo again. They did. They looked delighted. I nodded. 'You look like you're in love,' I murmured. The old ladies giggled. The sherry had made their cheeks pink. Pru put the photo back and Patti said musingly, 'You know, we've had fifty years of pastors, preachers and priests in this house, all experts on love they'll tell you, but you are the first to have noticed that.' The two ladies walked to the lounge together holding each other's arms for support. I glanced back at the photo again and took one last peek at Pru's boobs. Nice.

* * *

It was about that time that I really started to find the sermons hard work. It got even harder after it dawned on me that I was an atheist. Sundays used to involve an early start for me. I had to be ready for when the show began at 9, which meant 7.30am at the church hall. That gave us over an hour to put out the chairs and fill over three hundred thimble-sized glasses with red wine for the communion extravaganza after the initial sing-song and sermon. The band would set up while we did this. The preparatory church devotions were carried out to the thumping of drums and Peter, the main singer, saying 'one two – two – two' into a microphone. Peter had been something of a B-grade rock celebrity, making it onto the front cover of the magazines twice. Once when his band went to Number 1 on the charts and once when he overdosed on an exotic cocktail of party drugs and was photographed face down in the urinals at a city nightclub. Security cameras had recorded him entering the toilets at 1am and the bar staff were alerted to his condition at 1.45am. That's 45 minutes of men urinating on him in preference to disturbing their party long enough to go for help. A frank and emphatic commentary on the quality of his music. It's hardly surprising that he had turned to God.

We were a hand clappy, hallelujah kind of church. People would say 'praise God' a lot and when they shook hands they'd say 'bless you'. The more hip ones would say 'bless you brother'. We were a close-your-eyes-and-raise-a-hand-to-God-when-you-pray kind of church. The Sunday sessions involved lots of standing, swaying people with beatific smiles on their faces, the one hand raised, lips murmuring in prayer, being moved by the spirit of God or something. I suspect that this rarely happened without an audience. There was a lot of theatre on Sundays. And we were a church of healers and miracle-workers, a touched-by-the-hand-of-God-falling-backwards-into-the-arms-of-another kind of church. And we were a speaking-in-tongues-when-the-spirit-moves-us kind of church so a lot of babbling went on at the moment of falling backwards.

Sunday morning used to mean a congregation of otherwise normal people working themselves into a frenzy. An hour of singing. Music building up to a crescendo. Voices raised in prayer. And the devil used to get banished a lot on Sunday mornings. He was rebuked and chastised and ordered from the church 'in Jesus's name' but he kept coming back. He would be driven from Jonathon with the gout in his knee, in Jesus's name. He'd be rebuked for his part in Yvonne's cancer, in Jesus's name. He'd be ordered out of Barry's bad back, in Jesus's name. And each time, Jonathon and Yvonne and Barry would fall backwards at the touch of the preacher's hand, to be expertly caught and laid out flat, where they'd lie in convulsive prayer for a while, then rise and limp and hobble back to their seats looking well-pleased with themselves. But the devil would keep coming back for more, which is what kept us all in business. It would happen every Sunday. A sucker for punishment, Satan just wouldn't take no for an answer. So week after week he had to be rebuked afresh, in Jesus's name. Amen.

We used to tag-team the sermons, the preachifying going for a little over an hour all up, with music between each sermon. There were five of us pastors. You couldn't really say that we had radically different styles but different styles would probably have been frowned upon anyway, so we pretty much said the same things in the same ways. Have faith. Love God and each other. Don't commit adultery. Steer clear of wanking and gambling. Jesus was very kind and we should try to be the same. He died for our sins so we should be grateful for that. It was all pro forma stuff and I have to admit that sometimes when I was preaching to those people and I saw their radiant up-turned faces, I used to feel a bit of a hypocrite. But I always reminded myself that it was a means to an end and I wasn't really hurting anyone. After all, as I told myself at the time, I was only giving them what they wanted. Hope and entertainment.

After the Sunday morning session and before the Sunday afternoon session we would gather in Gregory's office and count the money. No-one seemed to think that this was a little odd but it was the quietest time of a Sunday. Heads bowed, and the susurrus of whispered voices as we counted softly under our breaths. Like prayer. Gregory had founded the church in 1987 and he was therefore the acknowledged *primus inter pares* of the five pastors. He'd sit behind his desk while we ranged our chairs against him in a semi-circle on the other side. Gregory had a big girl's bum. It was contained within a pair of over-tight trousers where it expanded to fill the available space. He was an expert on sin, constantly on the alert for the seven deadly ones, yet cheap Kmart shoes seem to have been acceptable in the eyes of God. We parted company on that one, I'm afraid. Our counting always ended the same way: Gregory leaning back in his chair, hands crossed on his lap, saying, 'Not good enough.' The Sunday afternoon sessions used to involve a lot of brow-beating as a result. Sunday afternoons always brought in the better yield. It was all a little distasteful I have to say.

But it was the point of all the hypocrisy. It was why this atheist played the part in prayer group, youth group and church. Because at the end of every Sunday, Gregory would call me into his office and hand me an envelope. My cut. A few thousand dollars in cold hard cash. I'd take it, go home and count it again, shamelessly. This was the pay-off. You see, it paid the rent on The Mission in Kings Cross. It paid for the clean needles. It paid for the abortions and divorces. It paid for rehab and hospitals. And it bought groceries for all those single mothers. If Gregory and my congregation had known where their money was going it would have been all over for me in an instant. They would have rebuked the devil in me and driven him from their midst. They would have thrown me out on my arse, and women would have died from dirty needles, children would have gone hungry, and unwanted babies would have been born unloved. It was a small price to pay. The fake prayer. The bogus faith. I wasn't doing it for me. It was my own exhausting gift. But if Gregory had known he'd have pulled out that Old Testament of his and found a curse in it that would have sent me to the deepest darkest hell.

* * *

While all this was going on, Mr Hallum was shooting blanks and Mrs Hallum was none too pleased about it. In one of our regular counselling sessions Mr Hallum related to me in a tone of horror and through the employment of euphemisms how he had entered a small white room in a fertility clinic and tossed off into a clear plastic cup. From his chair across the room from me, Mrs Hallum sitting meekly by his side, Mr Hallum explained to me in lowered sober tones that on that shameful day he had called ahead, being the good Christian that he was, to demand that all pornography should be removed from the masturbatorium prior to his entering it – a request unprecedented in the history of the clinic. The final prognosis: no baby without IVF. But Mr Hallum would have none of that. He was a good Christian, or so he told me, and apparently somewhere in the Bible IVF gets a panning. No more spilling *his* seed on the ground he had declared. The sin of Onan! Mrs Hallum was also comfortable with that, he told me on Mrs Hallum's behalf. He looked confident on that score but I knew he was wrong. I knew for a fact that Mrs Hallum was a *fucking* long way from being comfortable with it.

Mr Hallum, unique among my clients, used to insist on maintaining the formalities. He preferred to be addressed as 'Mister' and so his wife, by default, and in his presence, was always 'Missus'. He would baulk at calling me Simon. He was never good with familiarity, was Mr Hallum. My one-on-one sessions with Mrs Hallum, on the other hand (or Faith, as I called her when Mr Hallum had left the room), tended to be far more relaxed. Very informal. And therefore far more productive in terms of her anger management therapy. First, she'd suck my penis and then we'd root like rabbits. It was an altogether more satisfying relationship.

*   *   *

Around this time Evie dropped by The Mission late one afternoon. As she walked in the door she tossed me a chocolate bar and flashed me a smile, as she always did. She asked for a kiss good-humouredly, as usual, but didn't get one, as usual, so she slumped into the chair opposite me and raised her eyebrows by way of a conversation starter. Evie was wearing a short skirt and low-cut shirt and her boobs looked about ready to jump out of her bra. It was a device that would win her several hundred dollars over the next few hours but I suspect that even if she hadn't worked in the sex industry she'd have worn clothes like that. It was always nice to see Evie. She didn't take herself too seriously and she was witty and incredibly sharp. God alone knows why she had taken up prostitution but back then I believed that she would tell me one day and we'd nut the whole thing out, but I realise now that I worried about those things much more than the girls who stopped at The Mission ever did. They seemed to live far more in the present than I did. They were never sentimental about the past. The past was the past. It didn't haunt them. Perhaps that was a defence mechanism. After all, if your power of recall extends only so far as breakfast then you expunge all recollections of sex from dinner time the night before. No recollection. No burden. But without a past, the girls seemed to have had no yard sticks, no anchors. The girls I saw seemed to drift. With nothing to measure their progress by they became complacent and so when I asked Evie that day where she came from she just shrugged. Bathurst, she told me, off-handedly as if it meant nothing and was never a part of her. I asked what it was like growing up in Bathurst and she had no memories to share but bad ones. She told me it was fucking cold in winter, fucking hot in summer, all the blokes there smelt of sheep or engine oil and all the girls lost their virginity in the back seat of a V8 at the age of fifteen. I couldn't

20

help it. I asked if *she* had lost her virginity in the back seat of a V8. She shook her head and I laughed. 'Fifteen?' I asked, only half-seriously. She was losing interest, or feigning so. 'No,' she told me curtly. I rose and walked to the fridge for a coke. 'Well, I'm glad you made the age of consent at least!' Evie replied coolly, 'I didn't say that, Mister.'

*   *   *

A room full of silent six-year-olds is never really silent. There is always a lot of squirming and at least one kid full of snot breathing gaspily through an open mouth. That was the noise that I could hear at Sunday School later that week in the moments before Gregory told the children that there is no such thing as Santa Claus. I can still see those poor little buggers gathered cross-legged and exuberant in the minutes before he dropped the bombshell, their cheerful faces crumpling, the bottom-lip-quivering spreading like the Spanish flu, the quivers turning into sobs. When Gregory went on to clarify for them, stating with micro-pauses between each word, that 'Santa. Is. The. Devil', little Davy Mortimer's response was the most emphatic. He spontaneously voided his bladder. And so *I* was left to console the rest of them while Gregory marched Davy out the door and to the toilet. A Minister of Religion left alone with a six-year-old boy naked from the waist down! There was nothing to worry about with Gregory though. Mind games. That was more his gig.

After Sunday School was over Gregory returned to the classroom where I was quietly sitting by myself and feeling like a total prick. He moved heavily around the room, his big arse following him like a serious consequence, bending with creaking knees and little ughs to pick up the copies of *Bible Stories for Children* lying scattered about the floor. I watched him as he worked to build up a pile of books on the desk near my elbow. I didn't offer to help. He'd almost finished when I saw him bend, pick up a book, straighten his back and pause to reflect. After a time he shook his head and murmured, 'Regrettable,' for my benefit. I didn't say anything. He turned, looked at me briefly, dried his palms on his trouser legs, and lowered his head again as he thought something over. He looked very serious. He made his mind up. 'Next week ... *dinosaurs!*' he concluded emphatically and departed like he was really going to enjoy it. His arse left a second or so later.

*   *   *

I realise now that it was all building up to something. Everything around that time seemed to be taking on a new and deeper meaning. On the bus on my way home from The Mission one evening I found myself watching the sun dipping behind the city, my mind in public transport neutral. It promised to be one of those soft Sydney nights. I was still tired. I remember the bus slowed and stopped and the doors breathed open on a young woman who made her way up the stairs, paid the driver and walked to a seat just up the aisle from me. Anorexia. She was skin and bone. Her forearms were narrow and mean. The bones in her wrists were hard round marbles under the yellow stretched skin. Her hair was thinning and I could see the smooth dome of her skull. A death's head. A Jolly Roger. She was Auschwitz. Belsen. Everything about her, exaggerated. Big bangles rattled down those long arms and fat beaded necklaces weighed around her thin neck. She wore a short skirt and I could see the skin wrinkling around the caps of her knees. I averted my eyes. I couldn't bear to look. I was almost angry at her for her affliction. I gazed out the window again and my mind wandered. I thought back to when I wasn't always such a mopey bastard. I thought back to the night in Noosa when Susan, Allison and I rode our bikes down to the beach. I can still see them ahead of me on their rented bicycles, riding side by side, laughing at some stupid joke, leaning forward over the handle bars and pushing enthusiasm into the pedals. I looked back to the anorexic girl. I should have rested my hands on her head. I should have traced every bump and suture with my fingertips and purged her of the horrible demon, like some schmaltzy LA faith-healer. I should have told her about those other girls on the bicycles. I should have described

22

Allison to her just as she was that night. I should have told that poor skeleton how beautiful a woman can be with so *little* effort.

* * *

Days later, the anorexic girl was still playing on my mind. A world of self-absorption and of self-destruction. A world of appalling need and a world of greed. A perfect world for unequal exchange. It was Monday morning, 10am, and warm for autumn. Bright Sydney sunshine wearied the drooping gum trees behind King Street. In my little workers cottage I showered, dressed and gathered up my gear, not feeling so great about my fellow humans. As I closed my front door and hit the street en route to the bus stop, squinting my eyes against the glare, I noticed a woman walking towards me on the footpath. I was not in the mood. I could tell that she had clocked me, so I averted my eyes. She was maybe 48 years old, wearing a pair of denim jeans and a pink checked cowboy shirt. She was also wearing a white cowboy hat. I looked down. She was wearing white leather cowboy boots. They were a little over ankle length. But of course they were.

As we were about to pass each other the woman stopped, flashed me a big smile and said cheerily, 'What say you and me go up there and have some fun, eh?' She gestured towards the Tropical Sun Hotel, a breezy establishment on the corner known to obligingly rent its rooms out by the half-hour. I said, 'No thank you,' but she received my answer with ironic patience, cocking her head a little and saying, 'Are you sure?' in the tone that a mother uses when she asks a four-year-old if they've taken a wee before they get in the car. It carried with it the implied 'you know what happened last time'. 'Yes thanks,' I said and started to walk away from her again but she was persistent. 'Are ... you ... sure ... ?' she called out again after me with an exaggerated rising inflection and I raised my hand over my shoulder to let her know I had heard but was not interested. I guess she knew what she was doing. Perhaps there *are* men out there who really *aren't* sure whether or not they want to have sex with a 48-year-old prostitute in a cowboy outfit and it's only when they have been given time to reflect that they can make an informed decision. I knew *I* didn't feel like it but I guess you never know. Then I heard her one last time, calling out like a child with a lolly teasing her little brother, a siren's song above the swish of the traffic on King Street. 'I ... go ... doooooowwn,' she sang after me teasingly. I kept walking. I bet she did and I can't deny that the frankness of the offer didn't warrant some sort of respect.

* * *

I picked up the phone and called Mary. Donald answered. I told him that I had to rearrange my schedule and asked if we could change the time of our next session. I suggested the following day when I knew he would be in Canberra. He told me that he couldn't make it but thought Mary should be fine with it. He said, 'Just a moment,' and I heard him calling for his wife. A few seconds then Mary's voice. Very professional. Not a hint of desire. Yes, tomorrow would suit her. Yes, 4pm would be fine. What a pity Donald can't be there. Yes, oh well.

* * *

Mary was all languor. She would laze into and out of sex. Short high gasps after red wine, caresses, seduction. The climax was like an accidental outcome of another pursuit. Languid, big-breasted Mary. A body that had nurtured and nourished a child. A few pale stretch marks gave her tummy a certain authority, the same pale lines on her hips and the top of her swaying breasts. When she bent forward they'd form cones of soft flesh and the barely visible lines would radiate from the heavy nipples. Mary's body was full, firm, *womanly*. She wore it comfortably. After sex she'd often walk the room tidying up. She'd squat to reach under the chest of drawers. She'd bend to straighten the rug. I'd see her anus and vagina, her quivery wobbly boobs, the shaggy beard between her thighs. She didn't care. It didn't even occur to her to care because, she told me, a body that has carried a child cannot be embarrassed and because, as she also told me, it was *my* body by then too. She had made a gift of it. Its gurgles and aches were my gurgles and aches. So, dozing off the sex, I would see *our* wonderful bottom moving palely around the bed as Mary picked her clothing off the floor. Lovely. And when she pulled her clothes on, her bra and her undies, masking her hips and belly and nipples and hair, it seemed that *this* was the sinful gesture, the unnatural act. And you have to believe me when I tell you that at times like that it never once occurred to me that in sleeping with her I may have been doing something wrong.

*   *   *

The bedroom looked like a poorly designed movie set. A double bed with pink frills, pillows in the shape of love hearts, two policemen standing next to the bed chatting about last night's footy, and the dead girl lying on the bed in her knickers, face up, eyes closed like she was sleeping. I had been asked to identify a body. It was a young prostitute, maybe twenty-two years old, with long dark hair, a freckled complexion, over-red lipstick and a tattoo of a bunny rabbit on her upper thigh. To judge from the drugs paraphernalia by the bed it was an accidental overdose.

It was all a bit embarrassing for the proprietors of The Love Shack, a brothel with a reputation for being low rent and shady. The manager, a hard woman with deep vertical smoker's wrinkles over her top lip, said she didn't know the girl. Never seen her before in her life. She was lying of course. The dead girl was clearly working without papers, avoiding the tax man, and it could have cost the brothel its licence so they weren't being at all co-operative. As a result, the dead girl on the bed would be entered in the police books as a Jane Doe if I couldn't identify her.

As I walked in, the two police officers glanced at me but continued their conversation as if it was the most normal thing in the world to chat about the football with a dead woman on the bed in the corner. The poor girl. I dare say that she had suffered a few indignities on that bed but few could compare to this. I felt an urge to cover her nakedness. She was a prostitute but she

25

wouldn't have wanted these people seeing her like this. She would have considered it an intrusion.

The detective who had called me walked beside me to the bed where I looked into the dead girl's face. I remember hoping anxiously that it was not one of my girls. As it turned out, I didn't know her although she looked vaguely familiar to me. I'd seen her around the Cross perhaps but I had no name to give them. The police seemed faintly irritated. No name made it harder to wrap the job up. It was a loose end that they'd have to work late to tie off. We stepped away from the bed and the detective excused himself while he asked some questions of the uniformed coppers. While they talked in soft murmurs I looked back to the bed. The woman lay there like a stone. Utter stillness. There was no rise and fall of the rib cage. No twitch of the eyelids. She was categorically dead. She had made the grand transition from life to death alone in the bedroom of a brothel, head resting on a pink heart-shaped cushion. There's no romance in that death. You can't get sentimental about it. It was just a horrible waste, the absurdity emphasised by the bunny rabbit tattoo.

The detective came back to me and thanked me for my time. He paused, ran his fingers through his hair and tilting his forehead at the bed asked if I'd like to say a few words. It took me a moment to realise what he meant. He was asking if I'd like to say a little prayer for her, for the poor dead prostitute. I looked her over one last time. What would I be praying for? A soul? 'I think it's too late for that,' I said and noted for the first time in that room a look of surprise on somebody's face.

* * *

I went home in need of the comfort of a woman. The dead prostitute had left me feeling uneasy and vulnerable. After times like that I would always think first of Mary and her comforting warm breasts and easy calm manner but Mary couldn't make it so I gave Faith a call. An hour later and she was in my bedroom naked. Seeking comfort from Faith could be a double-edged sword. Her small body was a vessel for anger. Her pert pointy breasts appeared cross with me, her purse-lipped vagina seemed at first to disapprove. Her manner was mostly nervous energy, a slight tremble to her hands and cheeks, little tremours like a nervy Chihuahua. The sex act was a matter of dedication. Faith would *dedicate* herself to the attainment of the orgasm. Hers then mine, in equal measure. She'd devour my penis and testicles. She'd mount me, dismount me, push her fanny in my face. She'd grind her hips. She'd close her eyes like a child concentrating on a difficult mathematical equation. But after the sex her hunger would become more lovely by far. She'd curl against my body and nuzzle at my throat. She'd sniff my skin, inhaling me. She'd hold my hand. She'd hold my cock affectionately, dozily. She'd press herself against me. She craved. Not sex, but caring. Receiving it and giving it. If Faith had a sharp tongue or an angry heart it was not by birth or instinct. She used those things to defend herself against a world that had abused her. But I am fortunate to have seen the kinder Faith and to have fallen asleep with her warm racing heart beating against our rib cages. Kind Faith would emerge as my erection subsided.

Trying to erase the previous day from my thoughts, I lay on my back with Faith lying beside me and on me, one leg thrown over my thigh so that I could feel the tickle of her mons pubis and her smooth soft tummy. My penis was squished between our bodies. Faith hardly seemed to notice. She raised herself on one elbow and leaned over my face, warming it with soft kisses and a smile. I needed her. I needed female touch, a woman's lips and skin. Hallum was a fool. She could have made him very happy. Instead he broke her heart. Daily.

*　*　*

Another week or so passed and I found myself listening to Donna getting very worked up about homosexuals. It was Tuesday prayer group again. Donna had arrived early with another batch of scones and had taken a seat second from the front. That was always a worry. It meant that she had a bee in her bonnet. Tuesday prayer group was a great place for vexation.

Being vexatious, I mean. Sixty seconds after the two Carolines had finished the first session of sing-songs Donna had quoted the Bible on homosexuality, choosing to skip the parts that touch on love and forgiveness so as not to be distracted.

I watched Donna, over-rouged and thin-lipped. Face like a smacked arse. Her head was bowed over her Bible, a monster of a thing, as big as a telephone book and leather bound. She was flicking the pages with speed, pausing brief moments to bring her index finger and thumb up to her mouth where a reptile tongue darted out and moistened the tips. She was looking for more damning Biblical evidence. Poor Donna. I was tired and I tried telling myself that I was being hard on her, that she was not so bad. I'd seen her with her teenaged children. She loved them. The perfect mother and a devoted wife. You could always count on her to bake more scones than there was call for. She didn't have to do that, she was only trying to help, but she'd have died if she knew that every Wednesday the leftovers made their way down to The Cross, where they were consumed by fallen women who only charged an extra $60 for Greek.

That evening though, Donna was very unattractive. She called on the lexicon of hate. She used her most toxic words. Perverts. Aberrations. Deviants. Sodomites. They tumbled from her mouth like jagged little pieces of glass. I looked across at Sister Patti and Sister Pru who knew more about homosexuality than any of us. They listened to Donna with a look that is difficult to define. It may be that they had reached an age where the opinions of a Donna had ceased to have value to them. Or it may have been forgiveness. Later over nibblies I saw Patti and Pru standing with Donna, arm in arm for support, chatting cheerfully about scone mix.

*   *   *

Mister Theory dropped by The Mission a few days later for a chin wag. Mister Theory owned a bar-cum-brothel up the way named 'Cherry Pop'. He was very proud of the name and so he ought to have been. It's hard to come up with a new double entendre in the sex industry. That day, like every day, Mister Theory was dressed all in black which must have gotten hot in summer but I think he believed it set off his gold nicely. He probably wore a touch too much gold come to think of it. Bracelet, necklace, another necklace, ring. It was a case of conspicuous consumption, a bling fixation picked up after a year working as a bouncer in Las Vegas. He was with his off-sider Ed, a small man who used to hang on, and agree unreservedly with, Mister Theory's every word. That day Mister Theory told us how it is with people because, he assured us confidently, he had them all worked out. I had told him about the girl on the bus with anorexia. Nodding sagely he instructed us both (me and Ed, who was nodding his agreement even before the theory had been uttered) to take a look around us next time we were on the bus. Thirty people riding home from work. Thirty people all looking normal. Some go home to wives and children, others to friends and fun. But, he counselled us, on every single bus in every city in this country there are people who look as normal as you and me but when they get off the bus, put that key in the door and walk into their homes, they kick off their shoes and crawl into bed where they curl into the foetal position and await the coming night with clammy dread.

He could have been right but that seems like a lot of people and, as Ed pointed out, surely some of them just have a wank. Mister Theory wasn't convinced by Ed's helpful suggestion. Wanking would be treating the symptom not the disease he told us. But who am I to disagree with the theory? I think back on Mister Theory. He drove an expensive car. His clothes, though a little monotone, were of the expensive variety. He'd never finished school. He'd never read a book. But the money that paid for those expensive things demonstrated that he did know people or, at least, the weaknesses of a certain brand of them.

*   *   *

Another two Sundays of sermons passed after that which saw me treading water at the pulpit and going home to restless sleep. I'd been struggling for days when Patti and Pru diagnosed my problem: I needed crumbed lamb cutlets. They may not have been far from the truth. I arrived at their place in the early evening and could smell the lamb before I even got to the front door. I wafted in on old-fashioned aromas. Frying meat. Stuffy armchairs. Linoleum. Pot pourri. The two old ladies fussed around me all evening and I didn't mind it at all. In fact, it was lovely. Every pause in the conversation was interpreted as a cry for food. Slabs of meat were thrust onto my plate to fill the silences, all my no-thank-yous dismissed out of hand with impatient tsks. At the end of the main meal we launched into a bowl of homemade trifle, then a brandy big enough to kill a horse. And another one. Patti and Pru sedated me with booze, matching each of my brandies with a sweet sherry of their own. We were all tipsy when the conversation turned to my work at the Cross. Alone amongst my parishioners, they knew how I was spending the church's money there, and they approved.

In fact, Patti surprised me. She told us that she thought it would be quite exciting to be a prostitute. For a while, that is. She wished that she was young enough to experiment the way the young kids do today. I was sitting on a big round armchair sipping my brandy. The ladies sat opposite me, sharing a lounge. The arms of the chair were frayed and the stuffing was peeking out. It looked like they had bought it new about fifty years ago and they probably had. I must have seemed shocked by Patti's admission. 'Oh don't look so surprised,' Patti scolded me. 'I'm not dead yet'. Pru chuckled. 'We did our share of experimenting, Patti-babe.' They both laughed out loud, Pru leaning forward to slap the thigh of the only man in the world to have ever shared their secret.

Patti reminisced about her life with Pru. She said, 'Simon, I remember the first time that I made love to Pru. We had been taught that it was disgusting but when it actually happened it was lovely. Lovely! The next morning I remember feeling anger. I was genuinely *angry* with the world of finger-wagging, tut-tutting, God-bothering liars. That's how I saw them: as liars, as people hiding a glorious truth from me. But I've mellowed a lot with time. I actually feel sorry for the Gregorys and Donnas now.

They are tormented. They want the world exactly as they want it and anything else is an affront. Christianity has become a blunt instrument to them. They have deluded themselves into believing that shame and embarrassment can be bludgeoned into people, and love bludgeoned out. Christ has become an excuse for blaming. Blaming gay men. Blaming lesbians. Blaming, blaming, blaming. They think that they can use their mean and nasty version of Christ to impose their will. They're really little children screaming "do it my way". Throwing their tantrums. But I can tell you this much. They can preach of God from now till the cows come home, they'll never stop the fucking in Kings Cross.'

Pru slapped Patti on her arm. 'That's enough of that language,' she muttered tersely. Patti apologised. 'I just get so upset sometimes,' she told us. Pru rested a comforting hand on Patti's leg and finished her thinking for her. 'You see,' she said, 'the Gregorys and Donnas have never really *understood* sex. I think they see it as a kind of violence. In the Cross I am sure it often is. But not in our bedroom. Not in a loving bedroom. No matter what we do.'

Patti nodded her head in agreement. She concluded, 'Gregory and Donna over-simplify sex. They think that it can be tamed with prayer, controlled with strength of will and faith. But all this self-denial is so misguided. God gave you a prick, Simon, so why not use it! Just don't *hurt* anyone. That's where the sin is. The sin lies in hurting the ones who have shared themselves with you, not in hurting some God who surely has bigger things on his mind than which hole you choose to put your pecker into.' Pru gave Patti another cross look but didn't pull her up on the swearing. They offered me another glass of brandy but I'd had my share. I asked why, if they felt that way, they had stayed with the church. Pru shrugged as if it was obvious. 'Because we love God,' she told me.

We chatted quietly for a little longer and then I made my excuses and strolled home. As I left, Patti passed me a handful of crumbed cutlets wrapped in aluminium foil 'in case you get hungry'. Strolling home I reflected that my life at that time was

31

dominated by women. I was with the Kings Cross working girls most days and most nights. I counselled dozens of frustrated, depressed, unfulfilled wives in my role as preacher-cum-marriage guidance counsellor. There were my two lovers. And Patti and Pru. Women of all ages and backgrounds. Those with lax moral standards and the prudes. Straight and gay. There is something about all of them. An elusive, defining characteristic. It's hard to pin down but it occurs to me now, without any sense of crudity, that it is their cunts. It is their boobs. It's their big hips and bottoms. It's their soft bellies, their nipples and their thighs. And it is a keen *awareness* of these things. My body, my man's body, is a pale uncomplicated thing. My cock is an after-thought. It hangs between my legs or it stiffens. Urine and semen. Simple. But Mary and Faith and Eve and all the others seem to have a much more complicated relationship with their bodies. Their vaginas grow moist for lovers. Nipples stiffen at the touch. And they can cramp and bleed and betray as well. And the parts of their bodies that do these things can flick from sex toys to baby factories in the space of an ejaculation! And so my impression now is that, for the most part, the women that I knew were more comfortable with the *primitiveness* of the human body. And so it is rare, I think, to find a woman describing sex, as Gregory commonly did, as disgusting. And so I wondered at Donna, who used to find in these things such cause for horror.

* * *

Evie had her views on sex too, which is hardly surprising. One late afternoon, traffic growling past outside, she sat opposite me in The Mission focussing on the chocolate bar placed on the table between us. It had been there for ten minutes while she chatted away agitatedly. I could tell that something was up. She wanted to talk that evening, seemed worn out when she was normally so full of energy. Finally, she confessed that she just didn't want to do it that evening. She shrugged and sighed, 'Sometimes I feel I just can't fuck another man.' I knew better than to say what I was thinking. I knew better than to tell her then don't, just stop.

She would have just given me that look and shaken her head in wonder. Instead I asked her, 'So how *do* you do it?' Evie answered me readily enough. She explained matter-of-factly that she did it in all of the positions. I smiled at the confusion. 'No,' I said patiently, 'I mean how do you do it, night after night, with men you don't know.' Evie laughed. I thought that she had twigged to the misunderstanding but I was wrong. She explained, with the hint of a blush and a lowered voice, 'Well, actually, I think I find it easier than some girls because, just between you and me, I have a pretty big fanny.' She wasn't joking: there was a total misconnection. My question went to her spirit and her soul, the complex relations between her thoughts and actions. But Evie seemed only capable of interpreting my question in terms of her body. How do you do sex? She should have just said, 'With my body.' And everything else? 'With me.'

* * *

A passionate love gone stale, a painful break-up, neediness then despair. Yes, God got me on the rebound.

My relationship with Allison was a long garbled conversation at cross purposes, full of misunderstandings and unintended offence. It was five years of saying sorry and stumbling on in a state of confusion, not sure why she was angry, why I was upset, where it would all end up. There's no joy in looking back on a formative five-year period of your life and seeing that you can really fuck another person up just by being yourself. In fact, being the best that you can ever be! And yet interleaved with the pain and sorrow I guess we found room to be in love with each other.

What on earth convinced us to go to India for a holiday to patch up our troubled relationship? It's beyond me. Three and a half weeks beating away carpet sellers and tourist touts with my empty wallet. Tears and more tears and desperate, harrowing, love-making under slowly spinning ceiling fans. And me looking into her face, lying there below me, and seeing it set, and her jaw tensed, and her eyes screwed shut tight, trying to find something in me and in herself that was worth the pain and the heartache.

The emotion in our relationship was never more potent and visceral than in those hours of sex and after-sex holding. We knew it was dying. We were merely waiting for the cancer to run its course.

We ended up in Pushkar, a Hindu holy city in Rajasthan. A romantic location, ghats stepping down to a picturesque lake and two tall jagged mountains looming over it all. Pilgrims would come to the lake and bathe in its cleansing waters. Westerners would unsuspectingly drink the same water in their tea later over dinner in restaurants, too cheap to buy the bottled variety. A serene, magical, dysenteric place. The full stop on that clumsy five-year conversation. We had slept together in the afternoon. I don't know why. Afterwards she rolled on her side and willed herself to nap. I rose and dressed and told her I was going for a walk. She made a little sound in her throat to say that she had heard me but she didn't open her eyes. I looked back at her from the door. Her shapely bottom, her boobs cradled in the crook of her bent arms and her eyes closed to make me disappear all the faster.

With a heavy heart I strolled down to the lake's edge, past the cow with the genetic deformity (a floppy ill-formed fifth leg growing out of the back of its head, hoof and all, and his owner touting photos for a dollar), and found a quiet spot to sit and think. I had the ghat I had chosen all to myself except for an old Indian man in rags sitting about 15 metres away. As I walked to the water's edge and took a seat on the steps he called out to me in slow, drawled but perfect Indian-English, 'Will you give me some thing?' His beggar's cry had the tone of suffering and anguish. He gave voice to my own feelings of loss and need. But I ignored him. Over three weeks in India you become hardened to this stuff. In the mood I was in he'd need another leg growing out of his head before I gave him any money. A reflective minute gazing across the rippling lake's surface. 'Pleeeeease, sir. Will you give me *something*?' My friend again. I ignored him again. Then every thirty seconds for the next couple of minutes he'd try again. 'Please, sir. Something'. Then silence for ten long and peaceful minutes. A young pilgrim walked down the steps of the next ghat and stripped to his cotton underpants. He walked into the glassy cool water up to his navel and, letting his knees give beneath him, he slipped vertically down into the water, his head disappearing and reappearing again as he stood upright. He did this four times in quick succession, held out his cupped palms, muttered a prayer and turned solemnly before walking back up the steps and out of the water. I watched the whole performance as if it were for my benefit and I looked across at the old beggar who had done the same thing. The pilgrim dried himself and dressed and left us alone. Another five minutes silence then suddenly the old beggar's plaintive voice again. 'For God's sake,' he cried, 'Do *something!*' I did. I left the lake's edge and walked back to the hotel, to Allison, where we agreed to end it. Allison cried and hugged me but there was relief in her tears, mingled with the sadness. Three months later I was in a church praying. Nobody was more surprised than I.

* * *

Mary in the shower after sex: her soft hands move delicately across her body and I recall my own hands fifteen minutes before crimping her nipples, pinching, clumsy and graceless, greedy in the face of bounty. She turns her face into the falling water, eyes closed, head tilted back and turning again she washes between her thighs, lathering the soap in gentle motions over her groin and through her dark pubic hair. She reaches behind and washes her bottom unselfconsciously. More circles under her arms. With her hands she raises and lowers her heavy breasts, soaping the lovely skin underneath as I watch her from the bathroom sink, toothbrush in my mouth like a gormless twit. From time to time she looks up and watches me watching her, pauses, and resumes. I remember thinking, 'What in God's name does she see in me?'

* * *

The telephone woke me at 5am on a mid-week morning and I rolled onto my back and lay there for a few seconds in that unreal sunless light of dawn toying with the idea of closing my eyes on it. In the end I answered on the seventh ring and instantly recognised Jenny's panicked voice. Jenny from prayer group. Jenny, worshipper of the spiteful God. Jenny, abused wife, beaten with the bread board by a drunken husband the previous year. Her voice was a breathy whisper, a mix of fear and embarrassment, and I could hear her shushing one of her children gabbling beside her but the hush was a hissed rebuke, not soothing mummy-talk. She begged me to come over, pleading before I had even begun to respond and through the rush of sobs she whispered that Patrick, her husband, had come home drunk, and had collapsed in a stupor on the lounge. 'I'm frightened for the children if he wakes up', she told me. 'Please come. Please come. Please come.'

I dressed quickly and ran to the car. Twenty minutes later, the sun still low in the sky, I pulled up in the street outside Jenny's house in time to see her burst through the front door shrieking in fear. She held her youngest against her body, a small boy of three, snatched up from the floor and held like a sack against her hip, her left arm across his chest and his feet dangling. Jenny was running. The child flopped limply but his face was rigid with horror, his eyes wide and wild. Too young to understand, he had fallen back on the deepest instincts. No crying, just silence. As Jenny charged down the front steps she saw me at my car and, altering her course slightly, ran toward the side of the car furthest from the house. She was a mess, clothes and hair dishevelled, her eyes were red and swollen from lack of sleep and weeping, and she was barely coherent. I recall a moment frozen in time when her mind formed words and she gave voice to her fears. All she could say was, 'My Danny. He's got my Danny.' She pointed me towards the house.

Danny was Jenny's other son, a thin child of about seven, a quiet boy with patient suffering eyes and pale skin and blue veins. I turned away from Jenny and took in the little front yard. It was a picture of suburban bliss with a tricycle at the foot of the stairs and next to that a cricket bat. I opened the low front gate and walked slowly towards the door but halfway there I turned and told Jenny in a hissed whisper to call the police. She showed me her empty palms in despair as if to say, 'With what?' Before I could reply the security screen squeaked open and Patrick filled the doorway. Patrick was a big man, a builder with callused hands and a body hardened by aggression. He was wearing nothing but a pair of underpants all saggy in the crotch. He looked absurd but he still managed to scare the shit out of me. He looked me over with a sneer of disgust and levelled his hairy belly button at me.

'Hello Patrick,' I said softly. 'Get fucked, cunt,' he growled. I could hear Jenny sobbing from behind the car. I could think of nothing to say. I stood there for long seconds as the atmosphere clotted, then there was movement behind Patrick's hip and I saw Danny ease out from behind his father. He walked carefully through the door, down the steps, and trotted across the front lawn to Jenny who grabbed him by the upper arms and held him to her body aggressively. With incredible relief I watched Danny's progress then turned back to Patrick who hadn't taken his eyes off me. Drunk, angry eyes. I held his gaze for a moment too long, making his mind up for him. 'I'm gunna fuckin' *do* you,' he stated flatly and advanced down the steps.

The first punch caught me on the forehead, bumping my head so far back that I remember seeing the sky. I landed on my arse with my ears ringing. As I got to my feet the second punch caught me on the left eye. I saw stars and fell onto my hands and knees with the world whirring. I looked up to see Patrick ranging like an animal about the yard, searching for a weapon, something hard and heavy to hit me with, something to finish me off. A brick. A fence paling. But he had missed the cricket bat. I got to my feet and snatched it up. It felt beautiful. A big solid weighty thing. I looked at Patrick whose undignified saggy-underpanted drunken back was to me and it suddenly occurred to me that the fucker wanted to kill me. I felt the most pure of emotions. I swung the bat with all my strength, aiming for the side of his head, aiming for the soft part of his temple, surging with hate and anger and not caring if I killed him. As the bat swooshed through the air Patrick turned slightly and it smashed his nose across his face. He howled and held up both his hands. Blood seeped between the fingers but I was riding the swell.

I knew what I would do. I'd kill the bastard. I'd make him pay for all the shit that he'd ever made Jenny and her children eat. Her fractured bones. Her bruised eyes and crushing humiliations. He would pay for this with searing pain and broken bones.

I swung the bat a second time, bringing it down on his shoulder, wanting to hurt and snap and tear. I heard the hot breath knocked out of him and another howl as he crumpled to the ground. He raised both hands over his head, cowering on the footpath and I saw the soft bone of his bald patch and thought about it for a moment, the coup de grâce, but I knew I could never do such a thing. I let the bat fall to the ground and was about to turn to Jenny, was about to ask if she was alright, and whether the children were safe, when I felt a hot slash of pain across my face: the streaky sting of Jenny's fingernails as she attacked my eyes like a cat in a spit-fight. I reeled back in agony and as she launched herself at me a second time I caught her by the wrists. She writhed against my grip, lashing out at me with her feet, saliva flecking her lips but I caught her off balance and I threw her to the ground. She crawled towards her husband. I could barely see. My right eye burned where her nails had cut me. Tears streamed down my cheeks. My face was on fire where she'd taken the skin off in four deep slash lines, one for each of the fingers on her right hand.

Through the whole thing, Jenny had watched me from the car, she had seen Patrick go for me on the front step and punch me in the head, had seen me take him down with the cricket bat, and like a lioness in defence of her cub she had tried to wound me dreadfully. She had raked her claws across my face, gouged at my soft vulnerable eyes, sought to maim and blind me with a hatred that neither Patrick nor I could ever have dreamed of mustering.

*   *   *

On the following Sunday, Mary saw me at church. My face was red and sore and swollen. After five years of artful deception we came close to blowing our cover that day. Without thinking, Mary hustled across the church hall to me and in front of a room full of God-botherers she reached out her hand in a motherly gesture to touch and to heal my scabbed and puffy cheek with the tips of her fingers. You see, if there is one thing that cannot be dissembled it is the look of a person who wants to hold, and the look of one who needs holding.

*   *   *

Three days later Mary came to my place when her daughter was at school and Donald was at work. With hardly a word she held me and kissed me and took me to bed. We made love, Mary on her back, her left hand resting on my right shoulder, her right hand on my hip. She lay quietly under me as I enjoyed the warmth and sex of her body, her vagina as slippery as a peeled lychee. She encouraged me gently with touch and look as I thrust against her pelvis. As I came she accepted the shift to sudden forcefulness, bearing the weight of my body as the climax subsided by enfolding me in her arms. She stroked the small of my back. On reflection I remember that throughout our love-making she never once looked like coming, she never looked like wanting to, her orgasm not being the point of the exercise. Afterwards, she just held me and said, 'There there, Simon.'

Winter

ONE AFTERNOON ABOUT three weeks later, my bruises browning nicely, I started doing the rounds of the smaller brothels in the area. It was an arrangement brokered between the police and the Safe Sex Collective, a body dedicated to improving working conditions for the local prostitutes. Back then I was its President. I used to be greeted at most of the brothels by surly bouncers or pissed-off owners who would wave me in disdainfully and disappear into a back room. They hated me but they knew the trouble the cops and the Collective could make for them so they usually left me alone to tour the rooms and check for health problems and to interview the girls.

After a tour of one brothel I walked outside and stepped right in a dog turd. The perfect metaphor. I always finished those tours feeling unclean. All that copulation. What scents must the sensitive noses of the dogs have picked up in the Cross? I'd see them every morning on their walkies and again in the evening. It never occurred to them that they should regard the street hookers any differently to their pampered inner city owners. The working girls loved them. Every dog got its ears scratched and would be cooed over. They'd wag their tails with conviction and didn't care how the girls fucked or whom. I think that's why the girls loved the dogs so much. They were wonderfully non-judgemental and taking a shit on the footpath was nothing compared to the things the girls must have seen some of their clients do.

I entered the reception at Zanadu and found myself in a velveteen and shag-pile heaven. Velveteen-covered lounge in a room wall-papered with purple shag pile. There was a lava lamp on a coffee table in the corner blobbing and swirling lazily, an evocation of cum. The ceiling was tiled with little mirrors like those on a mirror ball. The effect was at once dazzling and gaudy and tawdry. There was a young woman behind the front desk which served as a chest-high barrier between punter and 'out back'. Mirrors, fuzz, lava lamps. I remember thinking that this girl must go home with her head spinning. The woman leant forward so that her elbows rested on the desk. She was wearing a low-cut tight singlet and as I approached she pressed her boobs together experimentally with her upper arms and almost went

43

crossed-eyed looking down her own cleavage. She looked up at me again and said, 'Aren't my tits just the weirdest?'

They weren't at all weird. She was. I introduced myself and explained why I was there. She nodded seriously, an acknowledgement of the worthiness of my task, but she did nothing. I looked around the room and she watched me look around the room. Silence then finally, 'So you're doing Craig's old job?' Craig was my predecessor at the Collective, an okay bloke but very Salvation Army. 'Craig was the *nicest* guy,' she asserted as if I might disagree with her. 'He never *once* tried to root Veronica!' This was stated with an admiring shake of the head, as if it really was something of an achievement, not trying to root someone. I nodded as if I had a clue what she was talking about. The girl gestured towards the door behind her. It had a little 'Staff Only' sign on it. 'Veronica's the talent,' she said. Another woman's voice called out, 'Ready!' from somewhere inside the back room and the girl behind the counter smiled, turned and ushered me through the Staff Only door. She had pulled off a neat delaying manoeuvre.

Before I could enter, the door opened and a man of about 45 eased his belly through it. He had the good grace to be a little self-conscious. He immediately assumed that I was a punter and as he passed the girl his Visa card he said in a quiet voice and a kindly tone, 'Go easy on her, will ya mate. Her daughter was in a car accident last Tuesday.' He patted me on the back. 'I know you don't need telling.' His card was handed back to him, he pocketed the receipt, slipped the card into his wallet, wallet into his back pocket and headed for the door. It closed after him with a scrape across the shag pile. The girl smiled at me again and told me he was a nice man, and I couldn't disagree. She went back to pushing her breasts together with her upper arms, head bent forward to watch the effect. She pushed them together, then took her arms away *very* slowly and watched them ease apart again. It was like watching a person trying to glue two things together when the glue really wasn't strong enough. They were pressed together once more and this time she held them, held them, and then pulled her arms away very quickly as if she might surprise them into staying together. The broad cleavage reasserted itself. We were both looking at her boobs now with equal fascination. I wasn't perving, I was genuinely curious to establish what effect she was trying to achieve. We watched them lift and separate one last time then she looked up at me, shrugged, and shook her head in amazement. I was pretty amazed myself. 'The work space is through there,' she said, pointing. I walked through and did my tour. There was only one woman working there that afternoon and I knew her from way back. We chatted about working conditions and she gave the place a thumbs up. Nice and clean. No rough stuff. I walked back out to reception and headed for the front door and the street. As I turned to close the door after me the young woman at reception smiled and waved. 'I'm Angela,' she called out with a cheerful smile. It was the most genuine and unaffected gesture I had seen in months. I waved back and closed the door with a hint of regret.

* * *

Four days later and it is Faith in the shower. She turns her back on the shower head, closes her eyes, and arches her back to let the water hit her forehead and wash across her face. By arching this way, she tightens and flattens her tummy. The hair between her legs is made sparse by the watershed, her labia pink and open in the hot water. As I watch, Faith straightens her back to stand upright again, and as she does so she brings both her left and right hands to her forehead, sweeping the water backwards in one motion. Her eyes closed, she looks like she is straining against herself. Her chin uptilted, her neck arched and taut, she pulls her hair back two-handed, like a rider on the reins.

* * *

I sat there thinking, 'I take back everything nice that I ever said about Donna.' I was in Gregory's office being scolded for what I was maintaining was just a poor choice of words and bad timing. He asked me to repeat *exactly* what I had said in last Tuesday's prayer group. He leant back in his chair and made a little steeple of his fingers. I explained that Donna had been speaking of homosexuality, and in particular of sodomy, when I reminded the prayer group of Jesus's words: let he who is without sin cast the first stone. I paused and shrugged innocently. Gregory looked at me sternly. After a few seconds he leant forward in his chair, choosing his words carefully. He took a breath and said quietly but firmly, 'You know she's saying you implied that she has engaged in *sodomy*.' He could barely bring himself to use the last word. I shook my head slowly and emphatically. A man unjustly accused. 'No, Gregory,' I said levelly. 'You know I would *never* do that.' Gregory looked at me a second time. He didn't seem at all convinced.

* * *

Evie the Prostitute on bodies: 'I used to hate the fat clients. The hairy belly buttons. The soft-tight tummies and their stumpy cocks underneath, like stuck-on plasticine snakes. The wheezing when they did it. But now I'm way better at it. I think it's because as I get older I see my own body changing. My arse is getting bigger. My tits are starting to sag. And yet, when I'm old and fat myself one day, I'll still be me! I'll still be sexy between the ears. I'll still want to do it with a sexy bloke. That's why now I don't just look at the bodies. I think it's more professional of me to think like that. I reckon I could fuck just about any man now.'

The last part said proudly. Evie looked at me. She saw something in my eye and reached for my hand instinctively in an effort to clarify a lost moment. She spoke quickly to reassure me. 'Oh, not *you*, Simon! We're friends!' She heard her own words, giggled uncertainly and half-laughed when I half-smiled. But it was at the same time both the loveliest thing she could have said to me, and the saddest.

* * *

I was lying in bed half-dozing to the sound of the shower's running water. Mary was washing away a morning of sex. I nodded off and woke up a little later in a yellow square of late morning sunlight, cosy-warm under a light blanket. Mary was walking around the room naked, little goose bumps on her bare skin. She found her bra on the floor and bent to pick it up. She looped it over her shoulders and settled her breasts into the cups in a business-like manner. I watched her as she searched for her discarded undies but before she could find them she was distracted by her shoes. They were brand new and she was *very* fond of them. Mary sat on the edge of the bed and slipped them on. They were black leather and very stylish. Naked except for her bra, she stood again and high-heeled to the full-length mirror in my room's corner. With her hands on her hips she swivelled left and right, the better to appreciate the shoes. She turned side on to the mirror and pointed her toe, front on and in profile, knitting her eyebrows. When she noticed me watching her she asked me if I liked them, regarding them carefully herself, her hands still on her hips.

I took in her creamy shoulders, the elegant line of her collar bones, her round thighs touching beneath the fuzzy smudge of her pubic hair. I glanced at her shoes. They *did* look lovely and I told her so. 'I think so too,' she said with a self-satisfied smile. She returned to the hunt for her underpants. When she spied them next to the clothes rack she bent to pick them up. As she did so I felt an urgent desire to hold her, to caress and love her. I rolled out of bed and lowering myself to my knees, I buried my face in the blancmange of her gorgeous soft bottom. She squealed as she unbalanced, righted herself, and surrendered, leaning forward, eyes closing.

*   *   *

My brief was to give a fifteen-minute sermon on faith and healing. Faith healing. I had been given broad terms of reference. Gregory didn't mind which parts of the Bible I used but he recommended (and there was no question really of me ignoring the recommendation) that I make good use of Lazarus and his famous against-the-odds comeback. Gregory reminded me of the salient points. *The* salient point. Lazarus had been dead so long that his body had started to stink!

Gregory used to decide who would give what sermon. He'd choose the topics every Monday morning and make the announcement in a meeting with his junior preachers on the Monday afternoon. Gregory took the responsibility very seriously, allotting the topics to us one at a time in a sombre tone punctuated with contemplative pauses. He would remind us that we were God's ciphers and that from the pulpit we were communicating the *literal* word of God. It was an awesome responsibility and one that weighed so heavily on my shoulders back then that I often found myself relieving the pressure on a Monday evening by going down on Faith or Mary back at my place.

Monday afternoons followed a familiar pattern. On that afternoon I sat in Gregory's office with the other pastors, teas steaming in our cups, Bibles on our knees. It was a pointless meeting really because we all ended up saying much the same things in our sermons. Graeme was given the parable of the Good Samaritan. Lucky Graeme: that was a great sermon. Really nice sentiment. Peter got Lot's wife and Hugh got Daniel in the lion's den. Me? I got Lazarus. It was a challenge, a personal challenge devised by Gregory. When he told the group that I was doing the faith healing number he held my eye provocatively. It was a dare and something that I had brought upon myself.

A week before I had gone to Gregory's office and had told him that I felt that I was not really cut out for the big ticket sermons, the cancer-curing sermons, the touched-by-God-and-falling-over-backwards-healed sermons. Gregory hadn't taken it well. He had been both affronted and hurt. He had risen from behind his desk, walked around to where I sat in my chair, lowered himself to his knees, clasped my hand in his, and launched instantly into prayer. 'God,' he implored, 'please help my friend and brother Simon. Give him the strength to see that he can save bodies as well as souls.' I sat there, Gregory's soft fat hand sweating into mine, thinking that maybe I had gone as far as I could with this malarky, but Gregory finished his prayer before I could finish the thought. He regarded me with eyes moist with tears. 'Christ loves you,' he said earnestly. Then softly, 'And I love you.' I eased my hand out from under his. It was a *very* awkward conversation.

Faith healing was the biggest call in the book and the sermon that I used to find the hardest to deliver. It was certainly the hardest one to fake. I never used to mind preaching that people should be good and kind and charitable, because that's good counsel, counsel that I would have liked to see given and taken more regularly in the Cross but it was another thing altogether to tell a gathering of people that in my Christ-enlightened soul there resided the power to cure them of cancer and clinical depression. That was a lie, a harmful lie, a cruel and ugly lie, and the sort of lie that raised spirits and then dashed them. A week earlier I had decided that I could no longer do it. But that was a week ago.

Gregory, like all church leaders, used always to be on the lookout for signs of back-sliding, the corruption at the heart of all disintegrating cults. By expressing reservations I was a threat, a splitter, a questioner. So after our little prayer that afternoon and after Gregory's gentle insistence that I should give the Lazarus sermon there was in his eyes a hint of challenge and at the heart of that there was recognition that failure carried with it certain consequences. 'We are a team,' he reminded me ominously: only team-members get their money. My money. Money to fund The Mission. The day the sermon topics were handed out I went home and thought it over. Without the money that the Ministry of Christ gave me, The Mission was dead in the water. No other charity used to come close to the sort of lolly I could raise in a week in the Ministry of Christ. Without that money, it would have all been over. With a wan smile and grave reservations, I had told Gregory that I'd give the sermon. He nodded approvingly as if to say, 'You have made the right decision, my friend', in the manner of a Mafioso.

And so, that Sunday morning I rose and shaved and showered with a knot in my stomach. I had spent three nights working on the sermon, flicking through my Bible looking for the juicy bits. Gregory was right. It didn't come much juicier than a stinky Lazarus, so I worked that in. Delivering this kind of sermon used to take a lot of eye-closing to rational thought and an acceptance that anybody in the congregation with an inquiring mind was going to think of you from that day forth as a dyed-in-the-wool loony. I left the house and hitched a lift with Patti and Pru to the church. They drove a little old two-door hatchback. I had to fold myself into a tight ball in the back seat but I enjoyed my drives with these two old ladies. There was only one steering wheel but they both drove, sharing observations about the speed and angle of approach of the other cars on the road. *Watch him, he's really moving. That red car is all over the shop. Traffic lights up ahead.* Together they navigated us to the church and came to a gentle stop in the parking area.

In the church there was the usual fervour before the fervour – chairs being set out, the musicians tuning their instruments in the background, officious people hustling down the aisles. The middle-aged men loved this time of a Sunday. It was why many of them bothered to come to church in the first place. The women gathered in small clusters in the seats waiting for the show to start and leaving the men to stand in dark-suited groups to speak soberly in deep manly voices about man-things. The unplanned segregation of the sexes was part of the appeal. Everywhere else in their lives, these men had to share the stage with attractive and intelligent women, pretend that they valued the opinions of the young, the beautiful and the amusing but *here* they were clearly the arbiters of truth and they had shiny tie pins that declared them 'Elders' as the proof. Amazing how much they loved it. Amazing how they puffed their chests out and shined those tie pins. And amazing how much the *same* those men used to be. They were all successful in their own way, but they were also, almost to a man, a tier or two lower down the career hierarchy than they probably should have been or would have liked to have been. A suggestion of a dearth of ability, hard work, ambition. It is hard to say, but they had a tendency to boast that they were graduates of the university of life. Some were from the school of hard knocks. They didn't like university students or 'clever' people. The word was applied as an insult. When faced with tough questions they'd recite trite answers. They were kindly enough but their kindness came from the cruel-to-be-kind school. They had no time for those that had lagged behind. The Lord helps those who help themselves, you see. Tough love. Prostitutes, mothers fleeing abusive relationships, young women carrying unwanted children, the truly down-at-heel, got little help from the Elders. They prayed for them of course but that was where the love ended: as a concept. If I'd had my way, I'd have taken back the tie pins. Of the seven deadly sins, pride is the killer.

The program for that day was a familiar one. As the congregation gathered and swelled, the band started playing softly. The handshakes and God-bless-yous were accompanied by the gentle unobtrusive sound of acoustic guitar, electric organ and the choir singing. None of it was in earnest yet. Everything said that this was just a social gathering, a place where friends could meet and chat, and almost as an after-thought, a place where they may worship their maker. Innocence. Kindness. Love trickling like treacle, and as sweet. It was what heaven would be like if it were run by an American corporation. We took our seats and Gregory rose. His big girl's bum made its way to the podium and without introduction or fuss he started praying. Gregory was an excellent pray-er. Bible in his right hand, eyes screwed tightly shut, he asked that the Lord enter this house and fill us with his spirit. Bless this house oh Lord. The congregation muttered, 'Amen.'

Then some announcements, practical matters with a Christian tinge. The knitting group would be meeting a little later that Thursday evening on account of Adie's cataract operation. There would be a seminar on how to run a Christian business next month and all men were encouraged to take part. 'All men': it passed without comment or thought. It was assumed. Then one of the Carolines was invited to sing for us, and she sang. A beautiful voice that soared to the rafters. And then we all joined her and sang for fifteen minutes straight. Music when we entered the church. Music now. It was an undertow, alluring and insistent. I looked around the hall and saw hundreds of people, glazed expressions, euphoric, soporific. They were happy, disturbingly so.

Graeme was invited to the pulpit and he strode to the front of the church with purpose. Graeme had a background, like most of us in the Ministry of Christ. Small fry really. A dalliance with party drugs in his teens and a brush with the law. Not a patch on Hugh who would speak later and whose childhood experiences with a paedophilic priest were truly horrible. I couldn't help but sense an over-compensation on Graeme's part. He was a little too eager to raise the subject of his past, his near brush with oblivion, his redemption through Christ. He was effectively saying, 'I was really bad, and now I'm really good.' Graeme craved to be a paragon. That's quite a way from humility.

We amened our way through the parable of the Good Samaritan, then elided into more singing. When Peter moved to the pulpit and delivered his Lot's wife sermon I felt that I was not alone in being confused. The moral of the story has always been a little ambiguous to me. Don't fuck with God? More singing, and then Hugh's sermon on Daniel in the lion's den. Hugh was a kind man, quietly spoken and dedicated. He spent whole weeks in remote Indigenous communities establishing schools and shelters for the needy. At the end of his sermon even *I* felt uplifted. The singing started again and as the choir led us, Gregory took up his position at the front of the congregation. Gregory and several hundred people raised their voices to God. Gregory's eyes were closed again. We all knew what that meant. As the congregation continued the singing Gregory raised his voice above the din in prayer. He called on God to move us, enter us, guide us. The hallelujahs were coming thick and fast now. Hands were beginning to be raised to the heavens. Parishioners began to sway. The music buoyed us. And as the whole production reached a point one shade below frenzy, Gregory signalled to the wings and the Elders moved forward carrying little velvet sacks into which we were to deposit our money. Gregory began to admonish us, cajole us, shame us, encourage us. The little sacks filled with cash. The music rose. Some broke into impromptu prayer. Bringing them down from this high had to be managed with care. We had to let them down easy, but not all the way. We had one more sermon to give. *I* had one more sermon to give. Gregory turned to the musicians and gave a little nod. They began to slow the music. The volume decreased. Gently, we were returned to earth, a suburb in Sydney's inner west. I glanced at Gregory and he gave the signal.

I moved to the pulpit, hundreds of pairs of eyes on me. I thought, 'I can't do this, I am going to tell them all that they are mad. I am going to blow this whole charade wide fucking open.' But then they looked at me with their *needy* eyes. They looked to me to give them something, something, *something* that would sustain them through the coming week, the next tedious, demoralising, soul-destroying week. I dipped my head and started reading. There was no extemporising. I read my sermon like a shopping list. I told them what the Bible says about faith. I told them that the Bible says God can cure awful diseases. I reminded them that the Bible says God can raise people from the dead and this is what the Bible says about Lazarus and about Christ rising from the dead. The Bible, Bible, Bible. I told them what the Bible says, not what I thought. They were all adults. They could choose to believe what they wanted. But I wouldn't tell them what I believed. There'd have been no point by then anyway.

I finished the sermon and Gregory leapt to his feet. He charged the stage and bear-hugged me. Turning to the congregation he cried, 'Come, brothers and sisters. Are you ill? Do you have pain? Do you need healing?' It was always surprising how many needed it. The music started again unbidden. People began to shuffle out of the crowd towards the open space before the pulpit. Gregory was ready for them. He rushed to meet the first, pressing his palm to the forehead of Maggie Parkinson with the arthritis in her knees and calling on God to heal her 'in the name of Jesus'. She threw her hands up and fell backwards into the arms of a waiting Elder. The congregation cheered like she'd taken a mark at the footy. More came forward and were met with the same response. Some approached me. They were in need of something indefinable, unobtainable. They came to me with longing in their eyes. I turned to Gregory as he turned to me, and he opened his own eyes just long enough to look threatening. And so I too was forced to rest my hand on the foreheads of the sick and the crippled and the maimed and the broken. They hobbled down the aisles to me in great numbers. They leant on walking canes and the shoulders of troubled daughters. They stood before me with their hearts full of hope and I rebuked the devil, in Jesus's name. I cast out the demons. I called on God. I made demands on his overwhelming powers. And as I did it, the music rose and swirled. It reached a new volume and a new tone, the drums and symbols rattled in my chest, the organ wailed. There was suddenly discord in the music where there had been harmonies before. My eyes were closed more than they were open. I was the perfect counterfeit of prayer. And as I rested my hand on the willing foreheads, people threw their hands in the air and spoke in tongues and fell backwards into the arms of others, and next to me Gregory was doing the same, casting out demons, perspiration beading on his forehead. Everywhere I looked I saw people falling backwards. Falling. Surrendering. And even I could feel it. This non-believer felt the overwhelming shift in the cosmos. A *power* had entered the room. A power that even Gregory had no conception of. It was the power of *us*. A room of *people*. A room full of beating hearts. A room full of *need*. And at least one man calling on a God he didn't believe in, casting out demons he didn't believe in, saying prayers he didn't believe in, and yet seeing people fall backwards at the mere touch of his hand. At moments like that, Mary must have stood in the crowd and wondered. With her own pale and withered child in the hospital, she must truly have despised me.

* * *

A couple of hours later and my adrenal glands were still throbbing. The church hall thronged with chatty people high on the Lord and profiteroles. There was God-talk all around me, freaking me out like never before. I spied Gregory by the altar. He caught my eye and held it, watching me with a strange little

54

Mona Lisa smile while I grinned with rigor mortis at the group of clutching ladies that had coalesced in my orbit. I couldn't fucking stand it. I was making myself sick. So I slipped away from the group and made for the back of the church hall, wending my way through the crowd to a door that led to the corridor which led in turn to Gregory's office. I took a look at my watch. In ten minutes Gregory would join us there for the money counting but for now I needed some me time. Another door led off the corridor to a room where we stored the spare chairs so I opened it and slipped inside. Thank the Lord. Quiet. Piles of plastic chairs almost filled the room and I took one off the top of one pile and sat it in the corner near the door. I rested in the cool dim space with my elbows on my knees and my head dipped for a weary half minute then heard a sound and looked up to see the door opening and Faith sliding into the room, leading with one rounded hip. She closed the door behind her and locked it in one deft move. I stood up uncertainly to greet her but before I could say a word she had pressed her pelvis against mine, rubbing her groin against me, her mouth to my mouth, her tongue invading my soft palate. I felt her lip-sticked lips tense and flex on the flesh of my own and her right hand tugging shamelessly at the buckle on my belt. She let my trousers down and reached into my underpants taking out my cock and milking it with her hand while she nibbled my mouth and buried her nose in my throat. I could hear the sound of chairs scraping in the church hall down the corridor. Voices filtered through to me as a muffled babble. I caught the echo of a distant laugh as Faith took the head of my penis in her mouth, her right hand still masturbating me confidently. There was no time for foreplay and no interest in it. Just the primitive act. Maybe a minute passed and I came in her mouth without shame, without scruple, with undiluted pleasure, copiously, half falling over Faith who was resting on one knee at my feet. As the orgasm ebbed away and as the world came back into focus we both heard at the same time the sound of Gregory's voice growing louder as he approached from down the corridor. Faith was up on her feet again in an instant, dabbing her smudged lipstick with a dainty fingertip and tidying her hair. I pulled up my trousers and tucked in my shirt hurriedly as my dick softened to innocuousness. Before I'd even finished re-dressing, Faith had the door unlocked and open. She leant casually against the wall near the door jam with one foot on the ground and the other resting on the wall itself, both hands behind her back as if we were the most innocent creatures on God's green earth. Gregory and Hallum were walking down the corridor together, deep in conversation. They had almost passed us by when Faith said, 'Oh there you are.' 'Oh hello,' said Hallum, stopping in his tracks and turning with school-masterly irritation. 'I really do wish you'd tell me when you're going somewhere!' Gregory smiled at me from over Hallum's shoulder and indicated with a nod of his head that it was time for the tithe-counting extravaganza. A surreal moment as we all politely bade each other farewell. As I followed Gregory into his office I turned for one last lingering look at Faith. I watched her walk demurely back down the corridor behind her grumpy husband, her hips swaying gently with each footfall, and the taste of my semen in her gorgeous little mouth.

*　*　*

One night in five years. Mary slept the whole night in my bed only once. I have burrowed a warm soft niche in my memory for it. The two of us lying on our right sides, my body finding her curve, my knees behind her knees, her shoulder blades against my chest. The scent of her hair. The gristly knuckle of my penis nuzzling against her thighs and bottom. Falling asleep and waking to find that in the night our bodies had become disengaged from each other, drifting on different currents, but always in the same river and never out of the reach of each other.

*　*　*

One Wednesday morning I was sitting in The Mission when David walked in. David was a nice young bloke in his mid-twenties, polite and occasionally spotty. His father owned a menswear store further up the street where David worked like a bastard six days a week. He'd pass The Mission every morning at 7.30 on the way to work and late in the evening I'd see him heading the other way, a physical wreck. His father worked him far too hard but David was such a good kid that he never complained about it. In fact, he used to tell me that he didn't mind the work. Not minding is not caring but he hadn't yet worked out that the boredom and the drudgery were at the heart of the problem we met to discuss every week. David was one of my Kings Cross clients and the only one that wasn't in the sex industry.

That morning David confided that he felt sad. All the time. Sad. I remember looking over his shoulder into the street outside. Pornography, brothels, drunks, drugs, hookers. Christ, who wouldn't be depressed? Before I could answer him, Mister Theory poked his head in the door but on seeing me with David he waved and called out, 'I'll come back later,' as he ducked back out into the street. David looked uncomfortable. There was no mistaking Mister Theory for what he was and what he did for a living. But Mister Theory was an expert on human frailties. In those few seconds he had summed it all up. 'Who was the virgin?' he would ask me later.

*   *   *

Faith knew about Mary and Mary knew about Faith. I was permitted the two lovers because they both accepted that they technically had two as well. Their husbands and me. There were rules. I never spoke of one when I was with the other. This rule was strictly observed, yet the women spoke often of their husbands. I allowed it. It was a form of expurgation, an assuaging of their sense of guilt. Rule: no love bites, no nips or nibbles. No marks that may show. Rule: no mention of children – the one that Mary had and the ones that Faith couldn't have. Rule: I must *always* wear a condom. Another rule: we were permitted no comparisons. It was Faith that had a tendency to break that rule.

For example, I am lying on my back and Faith's head is bobbing up and down on the end of my penis. She is dedicating herself to the orgasm again. This time mine. After minutes of exhausting work, she releases my penis from her warm mouth and lets it thump against my hollow belly. She starts nuzzling. Her mouth brushes across my balls. She gently sucks and licks. I feel her squishy soft tongue tickling and teasing. She goes down and down. I can hear her deep breathing. She pushes her face against my body. She nibbles and slurps and opens her mouth around one of my testicles. Her tongue probes and pushes. All the while her hand is on my cock, moving gently up and down. After I come she curls up next to my body and says very smugly, 'I bet Mary doesn't do *that!*' I am holding Faith in a two-armed embrace. She's warm against my ribs. I give her a short tight squeeze that says neither yes nor no but which seems to mollify her. But I say nothing. You see, Mary was rather good at it too, as it happens.

* * *

How did I feel when I was with the husbands?

Mary's man was weak. He was kind and good and generous and charitable but he was all those things because he was told to be so. It didn't come to him naturally. It came because he was preached at. Each Sunday was a goodness refresher course. He used church as a mnemonic device because his heart alone wouldn't do the trick. Nevertheless, I couldn't help liking him sometimes. He was witty and laughed readily. I could see why Mary fell in love with him. A handsome face and dark male eyes. But ultimately he was not a strong man and his weakness had poisoned Mary. He was a frightened little bunny. Too scared to ask for the promotion. Too scared to buy the expensive car. Too scared to make his mind up in the restaurant. 'You order for me, Mary,' he had said more times than she could remember. So she would order the steak done rare and imagine the red blood enlivening him and making him strong. He lacked balls and he all but destroyed Mary with it. When he was around she fretted and started and vacillated. Such a contrast to when he had gone away and we were alone and her hand would move surely to my face or groin and her body would resist as it was giving.

She would become another woman. Commanding. A goddess. So if anything poor Donald used to make me angry because he was bad for Mary. An energy leech. Sometimes I felt sorry for him. In my mind's eye I'd see him naked, preparing to mount his wife, losing control, cleaning up meekly. Sometimes I was angry. Sometimes I was sympathetic. But mostly I didn't feel anything much at all.

And then there was Hallum. I didn't like him. He was cruel to Faith. He had found the weaknesses in her and exploited them ruthlessly. He made himself big by making her small. He delighted in her nervousness and anxieties. When the menu arrived *he* made the choices, or worse, invited Faith to, sweating on the error that he could correct her on. The wrong sauce. The wrong wine. When Faith was with Hallum I'd see her looking into his eyes, always searching his face for the sign of approval, anticipating the chastisement. It was sickening to see her receive his approval with grateful relief. Worse was to see Hallum's chest expanding. Of the two men, Hallum was far the weaker. Our affair was a little revenge on him although that was unspoken. And although I too was using her in my own way, as she was using me, she never once looked to me for approval and I took her counsel, proffered after love-making, her small body nestled next to mine, as wise counsel, because she understood the world far better than any of us, because she had felt a little more pain in it and knew the value of kindness.

* * *

It's hardly surprising that Mister Theory had his own opinions on sex. What *is* surprising is that he was so sentimental about it. Like the day he told me about Marianne. Marianne was a paralegal in the city who Mister Theory had lived with for over two years. He was a clean-skin back then. No pimping. Just a straight up and down job in real estate. Suits and ties. Nine to five. 'She left me and she broke my heart,' he told me wistfully. 'I still see her occasionally, you know. I pass her some mornings on the way to work. She catches the bus on Cleveland Street and she's still bloody gorgeous. All dressed up in her work clobber. She was always very stylish, you see. Very sophisticated. Perfect complexion.' The memory pulled him up short. He fell silent for long seconds and I saw his eyes softening with something like sadness. A happy memory can do that. Finally he blinked the image away and mused softly, 'Life's funny. I sometimes look at that gorgeous, elegant lady – almost a stranger to me now – and think to myself, "I can't believe that *that* woman used to let me put my finger up her bum".'

* * *

I was sitting with young David again in The Mission doing something that preachers aren't really meant to do. I was telling him to get laid for fuck's sake. Actually, I didn't use those exact words but in a kindly and gently encouraging tone and with lots of reassuring smiles and it'll-be-fine head nodding, I urged him to get out there, meet some women, learn to enjoy their company, have some *fun* why don't you? I finished it all off with a paternal tap on his knee as if to say, 'I'm right there behind you, big fella'. He listened to me without meeting my eye, his body angled away ever so slightly. He seemed a little taken aback but mostly he seemed shit-scared. David's problem was a common one: he'd fallen for the propaganda. He hadn't yet worked out that women are not in fact all sugar and spice and everything nice and so he approached them all with a nauseating *decency*, petrified that if he flirted with them, asked one out, tried to kiss her, she would be mortally offended. He seemed to think women have sex by accident. That they don't actively seek it out, let alone enjoy it. How to tell him that most women actually like sex? How to tell him that with a man that they are comfortable with, a man that they really like, women will do rather a lot of things with him, without shame and without embarrassment, and sometimes in a pair of crotchless satin panties. You have to play your cards right though.

As David and I talked, Evie walked in and tossed me my chocolate bar. I caught it and couldn't help showing her how happy I was to see her with a big smile. She lapped it up. Good old Evie. In a tired and unforgiving world she still had some life in her, although she was getting harder. I could see it creeping up on her by the week. She walked past young David, a good-looking fellow about her own age, a man who should have turned her head, without even noticing him. The radar in her head that picked up punters like a big green blip did not activate. David was clearly no punter and never would be. It was those little signs that saddened me. In a few years she would be concrete. But David noticed Evie alright. He blushed, shifted in his seat, cleared his throat uncomfortably. He was fascinated but also mortified to be in the same room as a hooker and her vagina. I thanked Evie for the chocolate and introduced her to David. She nodded politely while David all but disintegrated with embarrassment but before we could take the conversation any further Gregory walked in off the street, followed by his big girl's bum. No-one was more surprised than I was. Gregory hardly ever visited The Mission. His charity extended to giving me the money to go there for him. We had a special place for The Mission in our Sunday morning prayers but Gregory kept his distance, finding it all a little unseemly. His defence was to overdo the God and salvation thing in The Mission. He started with a big 'Praise the Lord' and shook my hand with a hearty 'Bless you, brother'. He took Evie's uncertain hand and said, 'Bless you too, sister.' Her eyes sparkled. This was terrific entertainment. She looked to me and I could see it in her eyes. She was sharing the joke with me with one minute twitch of her eyebrow. Then Gregory turned to David cringing in his chair. Blind and blundering Gregory. Compare him to the astute Mister Theory, and Evie with the finely-tuned punter radar. 'And who's this?' he said to Evie. 'Your boyfriend?' David looked horrified. Evie saw the change in David's expression and in an instant the delight left her face. Suddenly she was a hurt and defenceless little girl. David may not have registered when she first walked in but Evie knew everything about him now, and what is more, she knew disgust when she saw it. In a handful of sentences Gregory had undone weeks of therapy with David and Evie, and had moved two precious young people closer to a tragedy.

* * *

One afternoon I penetrated Mary before she was ready. As the head of my penis nudged into her uncharacteristically resistant body, I felt her start. I stopped instantly, taking my weight on my forearms. I dipped my head, she raised her chin, and our lips met. We kissed for a long half minute, my cock nursed gently in Mary's warm tight vagina, and as the seconds passed I felt her body opening and moistening. I eased slowly back into motion, Mary beneath me, her eyes closed. But I am still haunted by the sound of the exhaled breath agitating her vocal cords at that first moment of penetration. A surprised low moan. Like disappointment.

* * *

Mister Theory was telling me about Donna because – and he was absolutely confident on this – he had her all worked out. I was not surprised to hear that all Donna needed was a 'good root'. Personally, I had always believed it was a little more complicated than that but Mister Theory was quite sure I was wrong. I played the Devil's advocate, pointing out that Donna had had six children so she must have known *something* about sex. Mister Theory was unconvinced. He sipped his beer and shook his head in the face of my ignorance. 'That just means she's had sex, mate, not a good root,' he assured me patiently. We were sitting in The Mission on a raucous Saturday night. The world was humming outside. Loud voices. Gaggles of young women clippy-clopping past in high heels and short skirts, leaning on each other for support as they laughed at their own stupid jokes. Mister Theory watched one group of girls pass The Mission window. All conversation paused as he assessed their arses. It was not so much ogling as a connoisseurial appreciation. When they had passed, he turned back to give me his full attention with a 'Now, where was I?'

His thoughts regathered, he gestured over his shoulder with his thumb in the direction of the girls. '*They'd* know a good root if they got one,' he said. I said nothing in reply so he expanded for me. 'They are up for it, mate. You can just tell that they'd go home and have a go. They'd *experiment*. No out of bounds for the right bloke. No hang-ups. No position too weird. No act too kinky.' I was still listening. 'Donna on the other hand. You can bet she gets in that bedroom and puts up the no trespassing sign. Plenty of out of bounds. No sex act beyond the conventional without some serious tut-tutting. I bet she makes her bloke feel like a pervert every time he gets a hard-on. But deep deep down, you know, she's up for it too. She's just too fucking scared. Timid. Too fucking hung up. Too fucking everything. And that's why she hates the girls that just walked past. Because she resents them. She resents their courage and their *freedom*. The freedom in their heads. But she's vain too, which is the real problem, so instead of her seeing the weakness as being in herself, she sees it in the others. And that Bible of hers? Well, it gives her everything she needs to salve her pride. It tells her she's the normal one when really she's just a mean little scaredy cat that can't bear to see other people having a good fucking time.'

*   *   *

Faith slipped downwards out of my embrace and I found myself standing in my lounge room with an erection, Faith kneeling naked at my feet. She took my penis in her warm hand and rested a moistened thumb on the swollen tip where she made tantalising little circles with it. Looking down on it all, Faith's grip and the cocked digit reminded me of the fighter pilot in the spitfire, thumb on the red button, all set to give the Luftwaffe a blast of the cannon. Also, there was the same look of grim determination as she leaned forward with a drawn breath and launched into a slightly over-frenzied hand job.

*   *   *

There had been no sign of Evie for days. One day, after a week had passed without her dropping by, I noticed one of her work mates walking by The Mission window. I jogged out the door and caught her as she was about to cross the street. When I told her that I hadn't seen Evie for a while and was worried about her, the prostitute sneered at my kindness. She was one of the hard ones, a smoker's voice and rangy drug-user's body. 'What do ya wanna know for?' she demanded, assuming I had other motives. I must have looked sincere because she finally conceded that Evie was 'hurt' and that's all she could tell me.

I feared the worst, imagining her the victim of some violent crime, beaten or in trouble, so I called in some old favours and got my hands on Evie's home address. In the early evening I went to her place and knocked tentatively on the front door. I heard Evie call out, 'Wait a minute,' from somewhere deep inside the apartment and a half a minute later she opened the door, standing gingerly on one foot. She rolled her eyes when she saw it was me. 'I might have known,' she scolded then turning slowly she half limped and half hopped into the lounge room with me following. I started by apologising. I told her that I'd been worried and I could see that in spite of herself Evie was pleased to see me. She put my mind at rest. There had been no beating. No rough stuff. She had simply sprained her ankle when she had slipped on a lettuce leaf on the floor at the local Woolworths. She watched me as I assessed her story for bullshit. She watched me with a frown, sitting on her lounge with her swollen foot elevated on the coffee table. 'Even prostitutes slip over sometimes, Simon.' I decided she was telling me the truth and we both eased back into the old friendship. She was right. I had gone there expecting her to be a victim. It rankled with her but she was also chuffed that I cared. She wasn't quite sure whether to be angry or grateful so she opted for smug. I asked if I could get her anything and she asked for a kiss, fluttering her eyelids and half puckering her lips. 'You're my knight in shining armour,' she teased.

It was the first time that I had seen Evie without make-up. I was surprised at how plain she looked. Not unattractive. Certainly not ugly. Just plain. She was just an ordinary person sitting on the lounge watching the telly. I'm not sure what I expected but I think I had expected a *prostitute*. A stereotype. The familiar one-dimension. I asked Evie if she needed any groceries and she gratefully gave me a list of the essentials. Milk, breakfast cereal, bread, potatoes. And she asked if I could get her a lemonade from out of the fridge. I walked down the hall to her kitchen and opened the fridge door. What do prostitutes eat? They eat chops and raisin toast and Milo. I took a can of lemonade from the fridge and strolled back to the lounge room where I became faintly aware of the absence of things. No framed photographs. No books, just piles of trashy women's magazines. There was a small vase of cloth flowers on the window sill behind the telly. Evie spied me looking at them. 'Horrible aren't they,' she said. 'They were here when I moved in and I haven't been able to work up the energy to throw them out!' She took the lemonade with a 'Thanks', cracked the seal and sipped. I sat next to her on the lounge and together we took in the soapie on the TV. Evie swung her legs around so that her feet were near my thigh and we stared blankly at the screen for a bit in the unfamiliar circumstances. We weren't in the Cross now, just somebody's lounge room. I was trying to think of something meaningful to say when Evie asked, 'Feel like a takeaway?' I found the menu next to the phone and placed an order, and twenty minutes later the food was delivered to the front door. We passed the next couple of hours eating and watching the idiot box, finding a surprising amount of clumsy silence between us. It confused me. I had expected it to be different, but outside of The Mission we fumbled for words and sought in vain for common interests. As Evie started to nod off I rose and wished her good night. She waved to me from the lounge as I closed the front door behind me.

Later that night I couldn't stop thinking about Evie. I had spent three hours in the home of a woman who knew sex like some people know fine wines. Strange, but there had been a moment there when Evie had begun to nod off to sleep, kinked on the lounge, her cheek on the cushion and her bare feet peeking out from under the blanket, and in that moment I had felt the need to caress her face, and to draw the wisps of hair off her brow and over her ear. I did not do it. I didn't do it because it would have confounded her. Evie could never have understood that such an impulse was not a sexual one, that I did not desire her, and that she did not arouse me. She would never have been able to understand that what I felt for her was *kindness*. And so back in my own home I found myself feeling an odd kind of anger for her because she had ruined something for herself and for me. By giving her body so readily to paying customers, she had cast biblical pearls to swine. Not her vagina. Not her breasts. Not her arse. Not her mouth. What she had cast away was the ability to enjoy kindness. Friendly embraces. I recalled that I had watched her sleeping for a while. In any other context, a woman surrendering to sleep in the company of a lone man is expressing trust but with Evie it had been cheapened. Her trust in me was valueless because she placed no value on her own body. In that house of hers, book-less, photo-less, trust-less and desire-less, I must confess that I had judged her, and had been disappointed.

* * *

Mister Theory, the pimp, on bodies: 'I hate it when I'm standing on the train platform perving at some sexy woman and a fatty walks up and gets in the way.'

* * *

At around this time a nasty trend began to emerge – Gregory took to casually dropping by The Mission unannounced, which made life very difficult for me. For one thing I had to hide the needles and for another I had to grit my teeth through more than my fair share of 'bless you brothers' and 'hallelujahs'. It gradually became clear that Gregory timed his visits to coincide with David's therapy sessions, and he was more than a little pleased when his visits coincided with Evie's. David and Evie would cop a full blast from both his charm barrels but the two young people used to respond very differently. David reacted like a needy son to a loving father, and with time it became clear why. He was a scared little rabbit and Gregory provided him with what he needed. Reassurance. A refuge. A place where he didn't have to confront his fear of women because in the church he was *encouraged* to fear them. How strange to see half our population as wicked things that will lead you astray! How strange to think of the beautiful things between their thighs and between their ears as instruments of the devil! But it was all fantastic news to David. Old Testament condemnations are music to the ears of a young man obsessed with sex and frightened by it. It's like telling an agoraphobe that they are *right* to be afraid of the world. Gregory was entrenching David in an awful position. At the end of every session Gregory would suggest that we pray. David responded at first with embarrassment but Gregory was a hard man to say no to and after a couple of weeks David too would bend his head obediently and close his eyes and say amen at the end of the prayer. I hated it. I had spent months telling David that he was strong and that the world lay at his feet. I had striven to build up his self-esteem and instil the confidence that life requires. Gregory's prayers and counsel did the opposite, as they were designed to do. All men are weak, he told us. He prayed to God to give us strength but David only heard that it is right to be afraid.

Evie responded to Gregory very differently, and Gregory tailored his pitch to it. Outwardly, Gregory tried the same tricks. He shook her hand with a hearty 'God bless you'. He chatted, with the Bible on his knee, all fatherly and caring. The first time she stayed for a chat, I watched Evie's face carefully. She was amused by Gregory. He was a freak show. When he left, she laughed. She shook her head in wonder that the world could accommodate such a fool. But Gregory was no fool. He was not so unlike Mister Theory after all. He too had spent years observing the weaknesses in humans. He had learned, through exposure to the broken and the demoralised in his congregation, how to locate and exploit the pain in people. So with Evie he came from a different angle. With Evie it was all about God's love. The church's love. The spirit of giving. The redemptive power of Christ. The love, the love, the love. He told her she was valued. And when he suggested prayer and Evie openly guffawed, he reached out and took her hand before she could say more and prayed for her warm, kind and loving heart, his head bowed and his voice ardent. And it was the first time that a man had spoken to her like this, and expressed passion like this, since she was about three years old. When Gregory left the second time, Evie looked uncomfortable. He had gotten under her skin. She wiped her hand on her skirt and said, 'He's creepy.' I could tell he had affected her. I felt impotent. What could I offer her to combat Gregory's beautiful lies? I could only walk her to the door, across the road from the porn store, and show her reality. Reality! A poor substitute for what Gregory could pretend to give.

* * *

At Sunday School my hypocrisy came closest to sin. A room full of eight-to-twelve year olds, and me forced to talk about God. I felt corrupt. I *was* corrupt. Towards the end of my time there I dreaded that the corruption would infect them. I had my reasons for my lies, my convenient rationalisations. After all, I was doing good work in the Cross. The lies and their money made it possible. But I also got a house because of it. I also got a wage. Deep at heart I knew that I also did it because it was easy. And when I felt that way, I worked myself harder, I salved my conscience by driving my body, telling myself that I was a sneak but still a good man, that my heart had its dark side but my actions redeemed me. All the same, sitting with the children at Sunday School, speaking of goodness and good men, I felt hollow, and after Sunday School finished I could often be found sitting alone, thinking. To Gregory and the others it must have seemed like I was contemplating the Lord. I wasn't. I was thinking that it couldn't last, and that *that* was a good thing.

* * *

Drunk. I knew it would come to this. I knew it the moment I walked into the pub with Mister Theory and through all of my lame protestations. I knew it the instant my lips touched the smooth cool rim of the glass. I *wanted* to get drunk and so a few beers in and Gregory and the prostitutes and all the stinking lies began to recede and next thing I knew I was laughing them off and all that mattered was Mister Theory's dumb jokes and the pretty women leaning on the bar at my elbow. Such a relief. I could. Not. Give a. Lazy. Toss. I had reached a kind of blah-blah-blah bar fuddle nirvana. I was incredibly amusing. Everyone was laughing at my witty observations. Girls were casting me flirty little glances. But best of all, I was happy for the first time in ages. I began floating around the room just under the ceiling, breaststroking through the wafting beer smells and garbled chatter and laughing. I was looking down on all the boys and all the girls and seeing things more clearly than I had ever seen anything before in all my life. Every shy smile, every furtive sideways glance, every girl sneakily reaching around and pulling her undies out of her bum, every bloke forcing a laugh at a dull one-liner. I could see it all. The embarrassments, the connections, the *everything* and I was wondering how it was that I had never seen these things before.

There was Mister Theory chatting to some drunken girl who was listening, but barely, to him trying out his tired old lines. I heard him say, 'I can tell. You work out, don't you.' I looked her over. She was wearing a pair of jeans that were so tight I could make out the finer details of her anatomy with such alarming clarity that I was genuinely worried for their blood supply. She had a plump and pretty face and a cheery giggly smile. Yes. But with the best will in the world I could not pretend that she might be a person who worked out. Of course, she knew he was lying. She *must* have known he was lying. But it didn't matter, did it? These were the rules of the game. It was a pub full of hormonal people staggering around half-hammered. In my state of heightened clarity I could finally complete the algorithm. I saw lust. And I saw loneliness. It worked when lust met lust, or lust met loneliness, or loneliness met loneliness. But it was only in the first one, when pure lust meets pure lust, when it is just cocks and cunts and nothing more, that nobody gets hurt. But lust doesn't meet lust very often. We are far more complicated than that. That's why there is a world of sorrow out there and that's why David was sitting in the corner, morosely slurping his beer in digestible mouthfuls, looking thoughtful and looking sad. I saw him before he had a chance to see me. I sobered instantly. I left the pub quietly and returned to my silent home. Bugger it. Bugger. Bugger it.

* * *

Every week I saw the knot in Evie grow tighter. It stooped her shoulders, bent her narrow frame around her belly. 'You can't do this forever,' I told her one day. 'I already have,' she replied lightly. 'Give it up, Evie. Get a real job.' 'I have a real job.' 'You know what I mean.' 'Simon, you don't get it. I *want* to do what I am doing.' 'It will kill you.' 'I am not a victim.' 'It will kill you.' Evie rolled her eyes. It made her look about sixteen years old. 'Simon,' she said, 'you can't save someone that doesn't want to be saved.' I let that pass in silence. We sat together quietly. Evie wasn't angry with me, nor was I angry with her. She knew that I cared for her and when I looked to her she returned my glance and smiled with closed lips. It was a gesture of affection, from both of us. I told Evie softly, 'I'm worried about you. You treat your body like it isn't part of you. You can't live one life with your soul and another one with your body.' 'You do,' said Evie, as quick as that.

* * *

Gregory would coo like a courting pigeon when he was with David. He spoke the language of seduction, coercive and strangely sexual. Watching him interact with David was like watching Casanova seduce a virgin. Her paltry resistance. His grasping palm on her breasts. The notch on the belt. Gregory was persuasive and patient and irresistibly insistent. He knew that the virgin would yield, because almost all of them do in the end, because in the end we all ask ourselves, what harm could it do? Would surrender be harder than resistance? And what Gregory wanted was for David to come to church. Just once. Just to see what it was like. 'C'mon. It'll be nice.' And David, for four weeks, threw up his weak defences. He was busy, embarrassed, Catholic. The excuse changed every week but Gregory wasn't put off. He cajoled and pushed. David said no but his eyes said yes. Finally, his excuses exhausted, David said that he could never go to the Ministry of Christ because his father would not approve, which is what the poor virgin would say to her Casanova. Gregory leant his face close to David's and rested a hand on his knee. He reassured while he subtly mocked. 'How old are you, David?' asked Gregory in a fatherly tone, and David told him he was twenty-three. Gregory inhaled through his nostrils but was silent. He sat up straight, withdrawing the comforting hand from David's knee and cocking his head sideways, once. He said nothing but he didn't need to say anything. He had found a young man, low in self esteem, unsure, uncertain, and found another weakness to exploit. That cocking of the head, a half second of movement, said, 'You are weaker than I thought.' Even the most timid bunny would have the balls to resent the gesture. So David said quietly that he would come to church after all. And Gregory ravished David.

*   *   *

When Gregory was with Evie he used the vocabulary of love but the grammar was all guilt and shame. He was relentless. He seemed to be at The Mission every second day around that time. At first he would drop by hoping to run into Evie but after a few weeks he began to seek her out. Finally he showed up at the brothel one day and asked to speak to her. She was mortified but Gregory would not be dissuaded. The first time she was frustrated but patient. The second time she told him to fuck off. Gregory responded with love, which he used like a weapon. He told her he would pray for her even as she told him to go fuck himself. He told her how God loved her and all the other fallen women. He dropped words like 'wickedness' and 'sin' and these are words that even the most hardened prostitute cannot fail to recognise as being in some way accurate, because what prostitute hasn't undressed for a man who has gone on to do wicked things to her? What prostitute has not washed the sweat of others off her skin at the end of the night and thought that here, somewhere in the sweats and fluids of these people, must be sin. It reeks. And sin reeks. Gregory was playing the waiting game. He was slowly bleeding Evie of confidence, self-assurance, self-reliance. He was putting weights on her shoulders. The weight of the judgement of loving and giving and warm and caring people. He promised that if she came to church just once then she would find love. He reminded her that Jesus went to his death for her sins. And hidden in the kindness of his words was the message that these people gave her only love, and she was repaying them with whoredom. At the heart of his message was the sneered, 'How could you?' A dangerous game. Especially when played with a person who has been abused by so many who have made the claim of love.

* * *

You should have seen them arc up when the competition was in town. The Mormons. The Jehovah's Witnesses. Gregory and Donna would trot to the front gate and sniff the air. Door knocking. Evangelising. It was one dog pissing on another dog's territory.

* * *

At 3am one Saturday morning I closed The Mission wearily, locked the doors and drew down the security shutters to stop the window smashers and vandals. There was a sign on the door for the drug takers. It read: 'No cash or drugs kept on the premises'. It was designed to correct another brand of human corruption. I dropped the keys into my trouser pocket and headed down Darlinghurst Road for the taxi rank. I passed two street prosti-tutes hunching their shoulders against the cold. One tried me on. 'Hello, darling. Looking for some fun?' I shook my head, too tired for their crap, and kept walking, my hands clenched deep in the pockets of my jacket. As I passed the entrance to a bar two men rolled out. We almost collided. I was about to apologise, although I had done nothing wrong, but before I could speak one of the men gave me a mouthful. I was a cunt. A fuckwit. I was lucky he hadn't knocked my fucking block off. I turned away and began to move on but he wasn't finished. He shouted out after me, 'Fuck you, arsehole.' He was a good half-foot taller than me and kilograms heavier. He was the tough guy though, with friend in tow, laughing him on. The anger welled within me but I kept walking – a combination of fear and self-restraint, but later that night I would fall asleep fantasising about turning, confronting, knocking *his* fucking block off.

At the taxi rank I stepped over a puddle of vomit. I opened the door of a taxi and eased myself into the passenger's seat. After I gave my address, the driver and I did not utter a word all the way home. Instead, my mind wandered. I assumed a position outside of all the shit that I had seen that day. It was a surreal perspective, accentuated by fatigue and frustration. I felt like I was seeing the world through the eyes of an outsider, with no claim to any part of it. I had forfeited my sense of belonging. As the taxi left the Cross behind and we drove down darker suburban streets, I felt my vision constricted to the breadth of our headlights. Everything outside them was black. I recognised nothing of this 3am world. Whores touting their bodies to men who rolled drunk out of bars, and picked fights with other men who had done nothing more than pass them by. A narrow street with nothing beyond it. A world stained by lights, not illuminated by them. A world without children.

My taxi turned the corner at the end of my street, and with the stink of the vomit still in my nostrils and the violence of the words uttered by the two drunk men still in my ears, I reassured myself that I was not a part of all this, but as we made the turn into my street, I saw the yellow points of our headlights rake across the window of my corner store, blank eyes reflected. I was behind them. A dark silhouette.

I wonder sometimes why I bothered. Perhaps I should have done what the others did. I could have drawn down the shutters for good and eased into the armchair comforts of the Ministry of Christ. I could have prayed and given tithes and given thanks, like Gregory and Donna and all the others. Which is to say, after all, I could have done nothing.

*   *   *

Three weeks since I last slept with Faith. I call her when I know that Hallum will be out. I ask how she is and she says with an exasperated exhalation, 'I've been *masturbating* all *morning!*' in the angry tone of the person who was on time for an appointment, confronting the one who has made her wait with, 'I've been *waiting* for an *hour!*'

*   *   *

And so it may seem that I had a good little thing going on back then. Mary and Faith and my lucrative hypocrisies, but I was still the sneak, and my house was still empty when I came home late and fell into my lounge chair, a television for company, and all the while the lingering fear that I would one day hurt both Mary and Faith by the fact of my desires. Self-serving to say it, but I shared a kind of love with them. It was an imperfect, duplicitous, stuttering love but we were all tied together tightly by it. Mary with Faith as much as I was with either of them. It could only end badly. I knew it. But I didn't want any endings.

They crossed paths on Sundays. Donald and Hallum on the church steps, shaking hands and chatting about business. Manly talk about figures and turnover. The two wives would chat too. They didn't hate each other but there was a fatigued tension to their bodies when they conversed. Smiles instead of laughter when the little jokes were made. Eyes looking at the ground more than at each other. Each woman seeing the other like a reflection. When they met at church I couldn't help noticing that together they looked ashamed. It was no fun being the source of shame, but how could they *not* see in the other woman the signs of their own actions? The betrayals by phone. The secret assignations.

The sex acts with mouths and tongues and hands and genitals. I didn't like it when they met. We all felt a little dirtier for it.

After one such meeting Sister Pru and Sister Patti approached me. They settled on either side of me and took one arm each. As they led me into the church Patti said, 'Simon, we worry that you're so *alone*.' Pru from the other side added, 'It's time you got yourself a partner. A person to love.' Patti concluded, 'Your *own* we mean, Simon. Your own.'

* * *

A cool cloudy Sunday morning and I was standing at the entrance to the church hall welcoming the parishioners. I shook hand after hand and traded endless God-bless-yous and insincere small talk. Out of the corner of my eye, I saw Hallum's sensible car sweep into the parking area. After a few seconds Hallum stepped out of the driver's side and a couple of seconds after that, Faith emerged. She looked unwell. I knew from a recent telephone call that she had an awful dose of the flu. She coughed into a tissue and dabbed at moist eyes as she hurried to catch up with her husband. Hallum was metres ahead of her by the time he had ascended the steps and taken my hand. I gave him a 'welcome' and he parried with a 'bless you'. Faith appeared at Hallum's side and she shook my hand. She was so tiny. Too tiny for the shit she took from Hallum. 'Good morning, Simon,' she said hoarsely. She was losing her voice but Hallum hardly seemed to notice. 'Did you bring the Bibles?' he asked abruptly. Faith gently patted her forehead, chastising herself for her forgetfulness. 'I'll go back and get them.' As she turned, Hallum sighed. Faith couldn't help but hear him when he said in his gruff school-masterly tone, 'Sometimes, she really is the stupidest woman.' My heart broke for Faith. Humiliated by her husband in the eyes of her lover. It took all of my will to stop myself from running after her, from taking her in my arms, comforting her, *enfolding* her. I wanted to protect her from this fool, and from all of the world's fools, and from any pain that our cruel planet could heap on her. But I held my ground and watched her crunch forlornly across the gravel to the car. Later she told me that she understood. She thanked me for my discretion, but how could she have seen my silence as anything other than complicity, and weakness, and betrayal?

* * *

Bored little Donna had been at it again so Gregory was obliged to ask me into his office and form steeples with his fingers. We were just clearing up the *facts*, he explained for me. He stirred a cup of tea on the desk in front of him while I sat like a naughty school boy in the ludicrous silence. Finally, the teaspoon was tinked against the rim of the cup and placed delicately onto the saucer. He slurped a hot sip, put the cup back down and asked if I could explain to him *exactly* what had happened at last Tuesday's prayer group. I cleared my throat deferentially and told him that the discussion had steered towards adultery, and that Donna had been kind enough to read aloud from the Bible on the subject. I paused for Gregory to nod his approval, a nod that also conveyed a fatherly concern. It was a serious nod. Then resting both elbows on the desktop, fingers steepled again, he asked what I had said when Donna had finished reading the sixth commandment. I stopped to think. I played it all over again in my mind but I honestly couldn't remember. I shrugged at Gregory and blinked blankly.

Gregory shifted in his seat and looked very disappointed in me. He told me in very clear language what Donna had *said* I said. He let it sink in for a few silent seconds and then moved straight on to the preaching. He reminded me that I was supposed to set an example, that God demanded no half measures. He told me in no uncertain terms that I should make things clear to a flock that looked to me for instruction. And all the while I agreed with him with little assenting noises. When he had preached himself out I admitted that I had been careless with my words and confirmed that it wouldn't happen again. 'No way. I'm sorry, Gregory.' Gregory nodded again. He was satisfied. I left his office.

On the way home, I chided myself for my stupidity and told myself I *had* to be more careful in the future. My error?

Apparently, when Donna had reminded the prayer group that 'thou shalt not commit adultery' I had given the impression that I was a bit wishy washy on the subject, affirming a touch off-handedly it seemed that 'we should at least do our best'.

* * *

I saw Faith again one week after her recovery from the flu. Kissing on the bed, I could still hear her husband scolding her on the steps in front of the church. I still carry the words with me as a burden. Like guilt. We made love without speaking and afterwards we lay together languidly. Although we both knew that Hallum would be expecting Faith home in an hour, we held each other tightly, warming each other in the cool of the evening, and in each other's arms we nodded off to sleep. Old and fond companions. When Faith woke at eight she dressed while I lay curled in bed under the blankets. When she was ready to leave, she kissed me on the mouth, leaning over the bed, the fingers of both hands in my hair. I glanced at my watch with a flicker of anxiety. Faith saw me do it. She reassured me with a pained smile and a resigned shake of the head. 'Fuck him,' she muttered and, threading an earring into her lobe, she left.

* * *

Later that week, Mary was sitting on the lounge in my tracksuit pants and one of my business shirts. She looked very small, legs folded up under her, book resting on her thigh, folds of clothing around her ankles and wrists. I was reading the newspaper, seated cross-legged on the floor near her, the broadsheet spread out on the floor boards. We were a picture of marital bliss. I was only distantly aware of the radio in the background when I heard Mary inhale sharply. When I turned to look at her she was smiling to herself, right ear cocked, listening carefully. She saw me and explained, 'I love this piece of music. It's from a very happy time in my life.' I listened. It was an unfamiliar classical piece, trickling tinkling piano. I watched her for a moment, oddly disconcerted. The music was an unpleasant reminder that I was a late-comer to Mary's life, that she had an identity before me, and would have one after me. I was surprised to find myself feeling jealousy, for the past of all things! A silly emotion. But I was also surprised to find myself hoping very much to be a part of her future.

* * *

Visiting a brothel one evening on another health tour I noticed a middle-aged man seated in reception. He had asked to see the girls. I watched with an odd dispassionateness as four prostitutes walked out of the back rooms, two of them chatting quietly. Falling silent, they paraded for him. They tottered in their high heels and short skirts and tights. They bounced on the balls of their feet in imitation of excitement, accentuating the movement of their breasts. They turned to show him their bottoms, laughing now and tempting him. They smiled and tried to catch his eye. They *tried* to be the one he'd choose, the one he'd fuck. The man assessed them coolly. He contemplated them with an expert eye and finally asked for the one with the big boobs. He actually used those words. There was no disputing who he was referring to. Diane grinned, took him by the hand and led him into the bedroom without another word being uttered. I saw his hand move to Diane's bum as they entered the room, and saw the door closing behind them. Proprietorial. An expression of ownership and power. But what would she do in there? I knew the drill. I had run the classes myself. First, she would check his penis for signs of disease – redness, discharge, odour. I pictured the man in the back room, all potency and power five minutes before, standing in front of Diane, sitting on the edge of the bed. He's still in his shirt. His trousers are around his ankles. His soft penis is out in Diane's fingertips as she turns it about, bending it up and down, inspecting with a serious furrow to her brow. He looks powerless. Like a little boy with mummy, his pee-pee poking out.

* * *

I was lying with Mary one evening after making love. 'I'd leave him, Simon, if I thought you loved me,' she said. I didn't reply, although by then I did love her. Some days she was the only thing that kept me going. I stayed quiet. To have said anything then would have unravelled it. To have actually said it aloud would have introduced all kinds of pressures. For Mary, I mean, not me. Besides, we both knew that it wasn't quite true. Leaving Donald would have broken her daughter's heart, and Mary would have made any sacrifice before doing that.

* * *

Faith one night as I reached for a condom: 'Simon,' she murmured. 'The doctor says it's not *impossible* that I should fall pregnant to my husband. If it happened, he'd never suspect.'

* * *

Mary the first time she made me come with her hand: she released my penis as the last waves passed and looked curiously at her sticky fingers. She tested the semen between her thumb and fingertips for a few seconds, then reached for a tissue. She cleaned her hands without a *hint* of distaste.

* * *

Another Sunday morning and I psyched myself for the day like an actor prepares for opening night. I took deep breaths before the mirror and got into character. Walking into the church was like stepping onto the stage. The lights would go up and I'd play someone else for a few hours. I'd adopt the mantle of priestly humility. I perfected my sanctimony. I worked my face into the rictus of a smile. I made myself a bland thing, bleached myself of colour, desexed myself. It left me withered and weak. Sundays used to exhaust me but they were also my most selfless gesture. A self-debasement for the good of two score of prostitutes, the bulk of whom saw me as something of a fool. But there were others that I kept alive with my health tours, clean needles, handouts and counsel. I paid for doctors. I bought new clothes for job interviews. I bought bus tickets out of the Cross, back to homes in the country, where the working girls could reconnect with lost families. I talked some of them off window ledges. I talked others out of murder. I bought groceries for their hungry children and sent others off to school. And so in spite of the hypocrisy I often wondered who I was hurting by my dissembling, when all I was really doing each Sunday was telling people to be kind to each other. I wondered who I was harming. Other than myself, I mean.

And so, colourless and bland, I ascended the steps to the church hall on a cool Sunday morning and said hello and God bless to a stream of the devoted. I was God-blessed endlessly in turn and I smiled my smile and shook soft hands. We were a middle-class church which means that our congregation's sins were middle-class sins: cold hearts, wife beating, coveting and alcoholism. And adultery, of course. A great deal of adultery.

'Bland' is not to say that there weren't expressions of emotion. At times in the Ministry of Christ we all stood at the pulpit and railed against iniquities but the railing was just an aspect of our blandness. It was trite. A hackneyed outrage, inherited from the prejudices of our fathers and mothers. Scripted in the OT. In a world of limitless emotion, their passion derived only from the baser instincts. Fear and contempt and disgust. More lovely by far is the passion born of love, and of the soft cheek of a woman, her gentle smile.

*　*　*

A milk line of semen trickled down Faith's soft thigh. The semen both a culmination and denouement. She seemed unconcerned as she rose from our bed, wiping it unselfconsciously with the palm of her right hand while she drew the sheet to her body with her left. She wrapped herself in its folds. A marvel to me. What could she possibly have thought that she was concealing from me? Her taste was on my lips and my semen on her thigh. I reached out instinctively and tried to pull the sheet from her body but there was a small tug-of-war as she resisted firmly with a kind of determined self-possession. I released her and gathering up the sheet again she left the room, clutching it to her breast. I heard her close the bathroom door. The whole episode, the rising, the tug-of-war, the exit, all carried out wordlessly.

*　*　*

A prayer chain. It was Gregory's idea. He described it as 'a mobilisation of faith'. Lucy Ferguson, one of the knitting circle, had been diagnosed with gall stones. In short, she looked like shit. Random and personal prayer did not cut the mustard with Gregory so he suggested that we dedicate ourselves to 48 continuous and uninterrupted hours of prayer for Lucy. Not all at once. Serial prayer. He asked for a show of hands. Who wanted to be a part of the mobilisation? But who would say no? Every hand in church went up. There were 'praise Gods' and 'hallelujahs' all over the place. My hand went up too. I was one of the preachers after all. What else could I do? Lucy sat in the second row from the front with tears on her cheeks. She looked worried. If she didn't get better now it really said something about her relationship with God!

This is how it was supposed to work. A list of volunteers was compiled, complete with telephone numbers. Gregory would commence the prayer at 9am on Monday morning. He would pray for Lucy for 15 minutes and then call the next person on the list. They would pick up the prayer for 15 minutes before calling the next. And so on. For two days and two nights. I was down for 7.45pm on Monday evening, and again at 11.30am Tuesday. Twice. That was Gregory's idea. We preachers carried a special burden. At 7.45 on the Monday I was standing in the kitchen peeling potatoes. As I started the second spud, the phone rang. Hayley Schiffer was on the other end. She sounded very *very* serious when she said, 'Pray for Lucy, Simon,' and hung up. I put down the receiver and returned to the kitchen. I finished the potatoes and cut them into pieces, then plopped them into the hot water in the saucepan. I set the fry pan on the burner and poured a little oil in the bottom. The gas lighter clicked and the flame took with a soft whoosh. As the pan heated up I took a t-bone out of the fridge, tore the plastic off its little tray and eased the meat into the hot oil. It sizzled. I sipped my glass of cordial. I checked the spuds. I looked at my watch. 7.59. I walked back into the lounge room and picked up the phone. The next on the list was Geoff Finley. He sounded embarrassed when he answered. I suspect he was one of the ones shamed into the whole affair. I said, 'Over to you, Geoff.' He thanked me, I hung up and returned to my t-bone.

A week later Lucy still looked like shit. She kept her appointment with the surgeon, had the gall stones removed, and made a full recovery, for which God got the credit. But sitting in my lounge room that night eating steak and mashed potatoes, I couldn't help reflecting that a congregation is a community, and a chain is only as strong as its weakest link.

* * *

When Mary spoke of it, she usually employed the anatomically correct 'penis'. In other contexts it was my 'dick'. Context: Mary lies on her back with her eyes closed and her legs splayed open as I kiss her between the thighs and tease her clitoris with the tip of my tongue. Sleepily she opens her eyes and reaches for my groin, asking as she does so, 'Would you like to put your dick in my mouth?' Another context: we have finished making love and in the rush of cuddle hormones I feel a pang of guilt. Mary reassures me with, 'But I *like* your dick in my mouth.'

Sometimes though it was my 'willy'. Context: I am lying on the lounge in my bathrobe watching the news on television. Mary strolls in, stands beside the lounge and watches the telly with me, hands on hips. A fancy takes her. She sits beside me and opens the bathrobe. I continue watching the news and my soft penis lies there warm and uninterested. Mary reaches between my legs and takes the base of it gently between her thumb and first two fingers. She wobbles it about with a look of curiosity, tries to make it stand up under its own volition. It flops back against my thigh. Mary rises and leaves the room, shaking her head as she exits and saying, 'God, willies are weird!'

Faith's vocabulary was more limited and somewhat less playful. It was unambiguously my 'cock'. The word was used in close association with phrases like 'I want to suck your' and 'fuck me with your'. It also found itself rubbing shoulders with 'pussy', 'clit' and in extreme cases 'cunt'. Context: I am sitting at my desk preparing next Sunday's sermon. Gregory is seated opposite, flicking through a dog-eared Bible, in an effort to help me out with a pithy aphorism. The telephone rings and when I answer it Faith's soft girlish voice breathes into my ear, 'I need your cock in my cunt … *tonight!*' Faith also used these words during sex. They made the act more potent for both of us. Where Mary seemed unconcerned about the grammar of sex, Faith took to it like a true etymologist. In particular, she enjoyed describing the act just as it was about to take place. Context: Faith and I are naked in bed, kissing each other on the mouth. We disengage by mutually understood unspoken consent and Faith half rises and turns so that her bottom is presented to me. As I rise to my knees and position myself at her rear in order to penetrate her moist vagina, Faith looks back over her shoulder, holding my eye, and says provocatively, 'Fuck me from behind.' As if I ever had any other intention.

*　*　*

Mary rested her handbag on the kitchen bench, rifled through the loose change, cosmetics and God knows what else, and finally drew her purse out. I stood opposite her as she poked through the coin pocket and I noticed the photograph that she had inserted behind the little plastic window inside the cover. It was a photograph of Mary and her daughter standing beside a horse. Mary's thick dark hair was bundled on top of her head, accentuating her slender neck and throat. She was smiling without showing her teeth, her arm around the child's shoulders. Her daughter was about nine years old. She was grinning at the camera, sticking her chest out cheekily. I could see the blue veins of her bald skull under the grey-pale skin. By then they had chased the cancer around her thin body for three years. That was the closest that I ever came to her.

*　*　*

Another health tour in another Paddington terrace house and brothel. As I slouched up the steps to the front door I passed two prostitutes taking a break on the front verandah, a squeally child with them. He was maybe two years old, roly-poly in a fleecy vest. They paid me no attention as I tried the door handle, knocking when I found it locked. One of the women was seated on a low stool, the other stood, leaning against the balcony railing, one hand on her hip and the other loosely illustrating the conversation with lazy gestures, a cigarette smoking between her first two fingers. As I waited, I saw the woman out of the corner of my eye draw on her cigarette deeply, tilting her head back to blow the smoke out in a hard white line that billowed at the end and up to the eaves. The child toddled from one woman to the other, wah-wah-ing to get their attention. They chatted away between themselves, largely ignoring the kid, touching him lightly on the head from time to time, an acknowledgement of his existence that did nothing to mollify him. As keys started to jangle on the other side of the door, I saw the smoker take one last draw on her fag end, an angry, needy inhalation. The seated woman asked, 'Are you working tonight?' The smoker was still cradling the last lungful. She shook her head no, then breathed the smoke out as she dropped the butt at her feet and stamped it out firmly. She took the child's hand in her own and with her other reached for the handbag resting at her feet. As the door opened for me and I made to enter the brothel's dim reception area, I turned briefly and glimpsed the seated woman open her arms to the child. 'Kiss for Mummy?' she said.

*　*　*

84

Faith sat beside me on the lounge one afternoon in her jeans. Dried to the denim was a milky smear like a melted diamond. She was chatting to me when she noticed it. She brought her thumb to her lips and moistened the tip with a little spit. Barely halting her chatter for an instant, she rubbed away the evidence of me.

*   *   *

How would they have known? Beyond the five senses, what could have betrayed me to them? We all felt sure that the husbands were in the dark. Mary in particular took the greatest care. After every encounter she washed before she dressed, soaping her body and hair, cleansing herself of any evidence of our love-making. Thus, my beautiful Mary always left my house smelling fragrant. One morning Mary dropped by my place. She was a little late. She told me that her husband had been late for work, which had held her up. As I held her to my body and kissed her, I noticed Mary's fragrant shampooed hair. Not for the first time. When we met, it sometimes smelt like that.

*   *   *

It was around this time when I hit the wall with prayer group. I can still remember the evening that Donna channelled God on the subject of beachwear. There was Donna flicking manically through her Bible, searching for God's injunction against bikinis and g-strings. Of course, she found nothing specific but there was always plenty for Donna to go on, and that night she was rabid. She railed against the 'shameless flaunting' of bodies on Sydney's beaches like it made a difference to something, somewhere. I listened but hardly. I was over Donna. I watched her thumbing through her enormous telephone-book Bible and wondered why she bothered. In truth, the scripture was irrelevant to her. She knew the mind of God already. As others took up the cudgels with Donna, my mind wandered in a get-me-the-fuck-out-of-here kind of way and I found myself daydreaming up the day, years before, when I visited Blue Lake on Stradbroke Island with

Allison and some of our friends. In fact, sitting there in prayer group, I felt like I did that day, only without the lake. After the itch and busy-ness of the surf and the terrible heat of the sandy path, and the pitch of the insects' shrill, the fresh water had seemed sensible and uncluttered. If the girls hadn't been there it would have all come off, but as it was the blokes stripped down to their shorts, the girls to their togs, and we lowered ourselves into the cool still water, the clarity of glass. Our feet kicked out at it lazily, the lake's bottom three body lengths below, visible down to the sand grain, rippled as if breezes blew beneath the surface. Dipping my face under the water I saw through the crystal the slender legs of the paddling girls, tiny air bubbles on their skin. Innocent and beautiful. That evening, listening to Donna droning on about the judgement of God, I realised how badly I needed that lake now. Life had become more than a little turgid. She was making my nice clean water all muddy.

Somehow, prayer group ended without me noticing. I found myself standing beside the table of cupcakes chatting to a middle-aged woman about school fees. She seemed well pleased with my company, rested her hand on my forearm, but it would not have been possible for me to care less. I was *a broken man*. I glanced to my left and saw Patti in the kitchen sweeping the floor, and in a gesture she composed my life. The swish of a broom and a pile of dry dust.

Spring

I T WAS A cool crisp morning at the university on the day that I was invited to give the first of three weeks of lectures in the Sociology Department. I was an expert on the sociology of seedy things, which didn't really make me especially proud, but it hit the right buttons at the university. I arrived early, around 9am for a 10am lecture, to make sure that I found the right building and met the right people, and so that I could check a reference in the library. I strolled through a cloistered courtyard and down into the library itself where I waded into a silence beyond description. This is what it must have sounded like on the Western Front when the guns fell silent in 1918. Not a human in sight. I checked my watch again. It was 9.15. I spent twenty minutes tracking down journals and then made my way to the Sociology Department. More stultifying silence. Two hundred metres away, beyond the borders of the campus, a city had been awake for hours and was humming with industry.

In the Sociology Department I met Shirley, the department's secretary. She was seated at her computer, fingertips resting motionless on the keyboard, her head turned obliquely so that her eyes wandered dreamily out of the window. She visibly jumped when I said hello. I suspect that it was the first human contact that she had had in days. I introduced myself and she told me where I should go to meet Professor Martin, and in an effort at companionable conversation I asked what she was working on. She looked surprised. It clearly bored her and it baffled her that anyone else should care. She told me that she was typing up the course outline for second semester. 'Isn't it the same as last year?' I asked innocently. Shirley looked mildly embarrassed. 'Yes,' she said, 'but I have to change all the dates.'

I walked down a deserted corridor towards Professor Martin's door just as he was approaching from the other direction, weighed down with environmentally-friendly canvas bags full of books looped over both shoulders. His eyes momentarily registered abject fear when he saw another human being within a 10-metre radius of himself but he drew with effort on his long-rusty social skills when I introduced myself, and managed to right himself enough to invite me into his office.

Professor Martin stood before me, hands on hips, looking very friendly. It was disarming. Actually, what was disarming was that I couldn't help but notice that he was wearing his trousers *very* high. The gusset had lifted and divided his testicles so that they were cradled snugly in two little hammocks of fabric either side of the seam. I couldn't believe that he considered that this was a *comfortable* way to wear trousers. He welcomed me 'on board' and suggested that we have a cup of tea before he walk me up to the lecture theatre. The Sociology Department shared its tea room with a variety of other departments from the humanities. Ancient History. History. Archaeology. The cramped room was crowded with academics when we entered. I looked around the room and took them all in. A frightening array of woollen jumpers with big cable stitching and worn elbows. If it had been summer I would have seen an equally frightening array of sandals and yellowing toenails. It made me feel good being with these guys: I felt very sophisticated. When Professor Robert Badgery, Head of Humanities, walked into the room, the chatter stopped momentarily, and as a sign of respect for the breadth of his learning one of the junior lecturers told him they were out of milk. In Oxford he'd probably be wearing a cap and gown.

We drank our tea over chit-chat and then headed to the lecture theatre for my first two-hour lecture. As I entered the room about fifty sullen late-adolescents made a point of not acknowledging my existence. Professor Martin introduced me and the hum of conversation gradually subsided, but only very gradually. My career highlights were distilled to a few sentences and all of them clearly failed to impress. As I rose to my feet and made my way to the lectern I was already thinking, 'Well, fuck them,' and as I began speaking I glimpsed Professor Martin exiting the lecture theatre at a rate of knots. I spent the better part of the next two hours giving the class my take on what makes a marriage work. And I should know. By then I'd rooted my way through a couple of them. Pens scribbled across pads, heads bowed and rose and bowed again at my words. And the longer that I spoke, the more I warmed to these young people. I began to remember what it was like to be that age. Virginal,

90

awkward, blushing, fumbling. One day I must make a t-shirt for them with a print on the front that says 'I'm full of potential'. I recalled that almost all of them would feel bad about themselves that day. 'Christ,' I thought to myself, 'Gregory would be in his element with this mob.' Those kids were *ripe* for the picking.

As I spoke, my eyes wandered the room. Mostly I saw just the tops of greasy heads and pens gripped in twisted fingers as they tried to write down every word that my mouth uttered, but one girl watched me calmly from the upper rows of the sloping auditorium. She was a few years older than the rest of them, dressed plainly in jeans and jumper. She listened more than she wrote, dipping her head from time to time to make a note. She gave the impression of being in control. She gave the impression, frankly, of being a shitload smarter than most of her class mates. She held my gaze when our eyes met, a little smile on her lips. And what kissable lips they were! She seemed vaguely familiar.

I finished my lecture and the students slapped their notepads closed on me with audible exhalations of relief. They shuffled out of the exits, avoiding human contact with me. As I gathered up my notes a mature-age student bombarded me with questions about references and theory and assignments. I couldn't answer most of them and she let me know how disappointed she was in me with a disdainful glance as she departed. I looked up to see the girl with the kissable lips. They were smiling at me. I smiled right back. The girl laughed, shook her head and said, 'You really don't know who I am, do you?' I shook my head. 'I'm Angela,' she said and extended her hand to shake mine. I took her hand briefly, shook and released it. I obviously still looked confused because she clarified for me without my asking. 'Zanadu,' she prompted. 'The brothel.' The penny dropped. It was Angela from the Cross, the brothel with the lava lamp and the shag pile. Angela who mesmerised both me and herself with the cleavage experiment. Angela, presumably, the prostitute. No wonder I didn't recognise her. She was modestly dressed, no cleavage in sight. Compared to the other girls in the class she was downright conservative. No nose ring, no belly piercing, no purple hair, no hipsters jeans with arse crack. She was just like anybody else, except that she worked in a knocking shop at Kings Cross in between essays.

As we left the lecture theatre together, Angela told me she was halfway through a degree, a double major in social work, and that her marks had been good. She said it with pride and cheerfulness, which was a welcome change from the surliness that had greeted me that day in class. Angela wanted to be a counsellor. She'd seen a lot of shit down at the Cross and she wanted to work there for a time, maybe make a positive contribution. She was articulate and funny with those enticing lips of hers. She told me that she was driving back to the Cross if I needed a lift and I accepted her offer. She explained that she was working the midday shift. Usually a slow time of day, understandably, but apparently there are men who find themselves feeling horny on their lunch breaks. Angela was walking beside me as she told me these things. She seemed less than impressed by these men but she had to pay for her education somehow, she told me.

On the way back to the Cross in Angela's car I found myself listening more than talking as Angela carried the conversation. She made jokes and laughed at them herself. She was open with her thoughts and feelings and curious about the thoughts of others. She seemed totally unconstrained. I couldn't help but think about the people I spent most of my days with. Emotionally constipated Christians who needed a Biblical reference before they could respond to new stimuli, and prostitutes who had long ago closed off the parts of their brains and hearts that allowed emotion to show. They had a bit in common, those people. Angela was a breath of fresh air.

When we got to the Cross Angela drove down a back lane and nosed the car into a small car park behind a terrace house. There was a sign on the back wall that said 'Zanadu Patrons Only'. As we got out of her car, Angela asked what time I'd be knocking off that night. I told her. She suggested that we meet for a drink somewhere but I found myself hesitating, just long enough for Angela to sense that I had my reservations. She raised her eyebrows very slightly, then furrowed them, then pursed her lips. In a slightly mocking tone she said, 'Don't worry, Simon. I'm not a prostitute. I only work at reception.' I felt guilt. Her tone shamed me. For all my friends in the Cross, for all the counselling, and for all the times I had defended their rights in churches, before the police, in council chambers, it still clearly mattered to me. I apologised with a shrug that could have meant anything, and we agreed to meet at a bar later that night. But I was already assessing the situation for the potential for embarrassment. It would be the leitmotif of our relationship, right up to when we met that night, got drunk, and went back to Angela's place for sex. Right up to it, and beyond.

*   *   *

One morning around this time, Mister Theory and I were sitting in a coffee shop near The Mission in Kings Cross when Mister Theory gave me his theory on Gregory because, he assured me, he had 'the prick all worked out'. The city workers had dispersed about 30 minutes before and Mister Theory and I had the street almost to ourselves. A council worker near the coffee shop walked from mangy path-side garden bed to mangy path-side garden bed, spraying some awful toxin onto the weeds. He carried a tank of the sloshing clear liquid in a container on his back in the way a scuba diver carries his oxygen tank. He walked bent at the waist to compensate for the weight, working a pump with one hand and directing the nozzle with the other. A fine spray shot out of it. It must have been wicked stuff. The council had provided him with a face mask which he had inexplicably taken off, hanging it carelessly around his neck. Mister Theory and I watched him work, sipping our cappuccinos as a fine layer of chemical poison settled on the froth and in the council worker's lungs. He didn't seem to mind. Finally, Mister Theory broke the silence with a full and frank assessment of Gregory's most prominent character traits. In short, he was a cunt. At least, that's how Mister Theory saw it.

I was a little surprised by Mister Theory's venom. He had only met Gregory a couple of times at The Mission, a quick 'bless you brother' and a brief chat. Normally I trusted Mister Theory's judgement but on this one I had my reservations. Sure, Gregory had his flaws. He was sanctimonious, he wore reprehensible shoes, but I had never thought of him as a cunt. Mister Theory reassured me. 'Believe me, Simon,' he said firmly, hunching over his coffee, 'He's a cunt alright.' I thought about it for a few seconds then Mister Theory expanded on his assessment. He said, 'Just look at that arse. Big and fat and soft. He looks like a fucking sheila. Do you think that *he* hasn't noticed? All his life he's carried that fucker around with him. At school he was called names for it. After school … My God, he's suffered for that backside.' Mister Theory paused to stir his coffee, shaking his head while he composed his thoughts. Conducting his speech with a teaspoon he continued. 'Yeah. This God business is all about compensating for his big girl's bum. What's it like hauling that fat arse around with you all your life, looking like a sheila but wanting to root them? You build up hates. You stack up the resentments. You start searching for ways to earn a little fucking respect, especially from the birds that won't root you! And what's the best way of achieving that? You find a way to scare them. You make yourself the mouthpiece for God. You threaten them with hell and you tell them that you hold the key to paradise, eternal life, that you and only you can teach them what they need to know to get to heaven. He's no better than I am, Simon. He's a pimp. A pimp for God.' Mister Theory paused, well pleased with that little analogy. He nodded to himself as if to say, 'Yeah, nice one.' He breathed in and continued for me. 'My punters want a fuck and I'm the conduit. You want to give it to some poor bird up the arse? Well I can arrange that for you. You want one that'll dress up in a Shirley Temple sailor suit and suck you off to Beethoven's Ninth, I can arrange that too. That's what a pimp is. You want paradise, mate? I can sort you out. Gregory tells you he can sort you too. He's another kind of conduit for another kind of blow job.'

'So you reckon it's the respect he's after? Compensation for the big arse?' Mister Theory considered my question for a microsecond before correcting me. He shakes his head. 'I was wrong about the respect thing. Nothing to do with respect. Not directly anyway. It's about power, Simon. Raw fucking power.'

I didn't say anything. Mister Theory looked me over then asked, 'You've never felt a little wave of it on a Sunday, during sermons, all those women looking up at you, big eyes, big tits, big everything?' I didn't respond. I didn't have to. It wasn't really a question. Mister Theory continued. 'It's about power and *domination*. Gregory is a control freak. He doesn't love these people. He wants to break them.'

I watched Mister Theory as he spoke. A few years before, I had seen a nature documentary about a troop of monkeys and sitting opposite the black-clad Kings Cross spiv I was reminded of it. The leader of a monkey troop is always a male and although he gets a lot of the rewards of leadership, including nooky and food when and where he wants it, the alpha male has to work hard for it. He's always on his guard against an up-and-comer. He has to fight for his position. Lots of alpha males die in gruesome fights involving teeth and claws. This particular troop of monkeys was led by a tough-guy alpha male. He was mean to the females. He bit them if they didn't do what he wanted. He demanded grooming but rarely returned the favour. And he was the toughest meanest bugger that you could ever imagine. He killed more of the other males than you would believe. All the females and all the junior males feared him but none of them liked him either. Then there was this beta male. He was quiet and caring. He groomed the females regularly. He shared his food with them. He defended them selflessly against attack. They *loved* him, but the alpha male resented him, recognising him as real competition. So what happened in the end? A fight? Alpha kills beta? No. An amazing thing. The *females* turned on the alpha male. They drove him from the troop, bleeding from his wounds, and the kind and caring beta male became the leader by mutual female consent. He cared for them, provided for them, defended them and in return he got all the little monkey ladies that a monkey man could ever hope for. That was Mister Theory. The beta-alpha male. He ran a Kings Cross brothel. He asked his girls if they would wear Shirley Temple sailor suits and suck to the Ninth, but they loved him. Deep down, he was kind. Well, kind so far as it goes. He paid well. He helped when the rent fell due. He never raised a hand to them. A real enigma was Mister Theory. Nine girls on his staff. He tolerated no users. No drugs. He paid his taxes.

As we finished our coffees, three men walked into the coffee shop and ordered espressos. Mister Theory fell very quiet. As they waited for their drinks they looked around the tables proprietorially. They saw Mister Theory and cast intimidating stares in our direction. Mister Theory said nothing and did nothing. As the men collected their coffees and turned to leave, one of them said, 'You'd better get that fucking money to us soon, friend.' Mister Theory remained impassive. When they had left I asked if he owed them money. 'No,' he said, 'which is what makes it all so awkward.'

*   *   *

On a yellow sunlit afternoon, trees swishing in a gentle breeze outside my bedroom window, the voices of my neighbour's children rising up from the yard outside, Angela told me that she was concerned about her vagina. Specifically, she was worried that it was 'too loose'.

I remember the conversation well even now. And who wouldn't? It's not every day that your girlfriend holds your eye and asks with tell-me-the-truth sternness, 'Are you pitching hotdogs down a corridor?' (That particular gem courtesy of the rude boys in high school.) We were lying in bed together naked having just made love. I was on my back and she was at my side curled up in my left arm with her cheek on my shoulder. When she spoke I could feel little puffs of warm-cool breath on my chest. I lifted my head a little and took a peek at her body. I mean, why not? She was lying on her side with her legs slightly flexed. Her pale bum lay just out of my reach. Its skin was smooth and enticing and squeezy, like her left boob which was squished against my ribs, the cheeky dark nipple pointed awkwardly up between our bodies.

I was composing an answer to her question in my mind, wanting to reassure her, but how do you tell a woman that her vagina is sublime? I recall her urgent pink mouth exploring and teasing. I thought of the moment of willing consent, the surrender without being abject or needy, and that wonderful moment when she had lain back and opened her legs, raising her knees, shifting her pelvis. And the perfect perfect perfect moment of penetration. Leaning into her warm slippery body. Like melted butter. Sublime.

Then I considered my own body. From where I was, head tilted on my pillow, I could see its full length. Bony ribs. Nipples fringed by a clown's wig of ridiculous hairs. But it was worse than that. Lying next to Angela's curvaceous body my own seemed pale and thin and utilitarian, a machine for gurgling food. My vaguely tumescent penis had thrown itself nonchalantly across my right groin. It looked like a pink sea cucumber washed into the shallows. There was something about the angle at which it was lying there like a brute that reminded me of a drunk leaning against a bar. Can I buy you a drink darling? Pretty disgusting really and yet not fifteen minutes before, Angela had nursed it in her sweet innocent mouth.

Her vagina? My God, I could have written poems about her vagina. A fucking haiku. But it came out as, 'Your fanny is *lovely*, darling.' That sounded a little lame so I rolled over and kissed her on the mouth. Angela turned her face to me and met my lips with hers but sometimes it takes more than a kiss to be reassuring.

*   *   *

Tuesday prayer group. For the first time in five years there was no Sister Patti or Sister Pru. Donna told me that Pru had been unwell and Patti was staying home to keep her company. We spent the evening at prayer group covering old ground (something about Samaritans, virgins or wrath, I'm guessing), then wrapped the session up with Donna leading us through a prayer for the starving children in the Sudan. We then gorged ourselves on scones and whipped cream. Without Patti and Pru, I was left to clean up on my own. I rinsed the dishes and stacked the chairs and couldn't help but miss the old ladies who were such good company. Then, unable to contain my concern, I made the short trip around to their house. Patti answered the door in Pru's snaggy blue cardigan. She took my hand and led me into the lounge room where Pru was sitting on the fat sofa under an enormous doona, her little head poking out the top. She smiled when she saw me and a hand emerged from the curves of the doona to give me a wave. I was passed a brandy before I had even sat down.

Patti was very fussy that night. She hovered around Pru, fluffing pillows and refilling tea cups. I asked what the problem was as Pru slapped Patti's hand away in irritation. 'What's wrong?' she repeated, 'I'm old is what's wrong.' Patti interrupted. 'The doctor says she needs tests, Simon. She just won't take a doctor's orders!' 'I'm fine,' snapped Pru and pulled her arms out from under the doona in order to cross them across her chest in frustration, but I could tell that Patti might have good reason to be worried. Pru looked drawn and pale. She had lost weight in the week since I had last seen her. There was something not quite right. I looked to Patti who looked very worried. 'What sort of tests?' I asked fearfully. Pru didn't answer. She looked quite angry about the whole thing, so I turned again to Patti. There was genuine concern in her eye. 'Cancer,' she told me in barely more than a whisper.

* * *

And yet I was happy! Deliriously happy. The happiest that I had been in years, and I had Angela to thank for it. She had had a sudden, unexpected and uplifting effect on me. She was full of energy, enthusiasm, humour and lust. She made me laugh, blasted away the dark thoughts with the light of her smile. She energised me. She threw herself into my arms when we met, teased me, tickled me unashamedly. It made me feel desirable, masculine, sexy, like a young man discovering his first love. And best of all, she was not married. I had only *her* to think about, and she thought only of me. So uncomplicated after my affairs of the last few years. That first week or two of our relationship, I walked through the Cross in the mornings on the way to work, cars and trucks grumbling past me and belching shit out of their exhaust pipes, and I was breathing nothing but the clean, fresh air of a dewy meadow.

But then, people can get used to just about anything. At around this time, one morning I was strolling down a lane behind King Street in Newtown when I passed a grease-trap man emptying the unspeakable filth of a corrupt city out of the sewers of a block of units. A battered truck with a big round tank on the back was connected to a hole in the ground by a throbbing murmuring pipe. A cloud of gag-making stink hovered over the truck, and at its epicentre stood the grease-trap man dressed in blue tracky daks and a t-shirt smeared with sewer goop. He watched my approach impassively, foul vapours wafting around him, munching casually on a Mars Bar. Yes. A Mars Bar.

That's people. Adaptable. There are some women who have gotten used to men taking a wee in their mouths. There are others that have gotten used to undressing, bending over and letting men insert dildos the size of the Hindenberg in their backsides. I know this because later that evening I found myself perusing the newly installed porn shelves in the Zanadu waiting room with Angela standing behind me watching with a look of surprisingly prudish disapproval on her face. *Dumpin' Doughnuts* caught my eye. There was an image on the front cover that beggars description. I turned to Angela ready to make some unfunny joke but she was not impressed. She looked away and I put the DVD back on the shelf guiltily. I moved over to her and gave her a big stupid hug. I shook her around teasingly. She let me do it. She didn't resist. But she didn't kiss me either.

* * *

And then I finally met Veronica, Veronica the Talent, and I must admit that I was a little surprised. I don't know what I was expecting but I do know that I *wasn't* expecting a 48-year-old woman in a lycra bodysuit to walk out from behind the Staff Only door scrubbing her tongue with a toothbrush. The effect certainly didn't turn my mind to the sex act but Veronica took one look at me and assumed that I was a punter. With barely a glance she stopped scrubbing and said through a mouthful of toothpaste, 'Take a seat, sweetie. I'll be with you in a tick.' She turned and passed back through the Staff Only door leaving Angela and me alone again. 'I really respect that lady,' said Angela with great seriousness. 'She's a very strong woman.' And good with oral hygiene, I almost ventured, but thought better of it. Angela walked inside to tell Veronica that I didn't want to sleep with her and she came back out all smiles and shook my hand. I could feel the small bones and the thin cool skin. She didn't feel very strong. Quite the opposite. She looked brittle, breakable. When she laughed, it sounded angry. You could tell she'd seen her fair share of the worst of men and it had left her more than a little jaded. When Angela told Veronica that I was her boyfriend, Veronica looked at me almost sadly. 'Look after her,' she cautioned. She didn't look like she believed me when I said I would. Veronica glanced at the clock barely visible on the shag-pile wall opposite and told Angela she was calling it a night. She asked Angela to lock up and disappeared behind the door again, emerging a half-minute later in a prim trench coat. Veronica slung her handbag over her shoulder and headed for the door. 'Nice to meet you,' she called out as she left the shop and disappeared down the street like any other woman.

When we were alone, Angela invited me into the *sanctum sanctissimus*. She took my hand and led me into Veronica's work area. I'd glimpsed it before in my health tours but this time I had unfettered access. A surprisingly normal hallway (a couple of vaguely erotic nudes on the wall) and a single room featuring a sole double bed. No windows. A lot of frills and fluffy pink things, presumably a tilt at femininity strictly for the benefit of the punters to judge by Veronica's jaundiced eye. Angela went to the side of the bed, leant over it and in sweeping arcs brushed down the creases in the bedspread with the palm of her hand. It was a fussy domestic gesture that seemed wholly out of place here, on this bed, where hundreds of men had done the dirty with Veronica.

There was a little bathroom at the far end of the room. Angela went in and checked it for neatness. As she flicked the light on I noticed the gaudy wallpaper. Naked women with impossibly pointy tits, eyes closed in ecstasy, excited by some invisible force. Angela wiped the sink down without even noticing them. I recalled the afternoon that we first met and her cleavage fixation. This had to be working on her at some level. There was a bedside table opposite me. I walked around the bed and opened the drawer, taking in the sordid contents: a bowl of condoms, a bright pink dildo and an enormous lubricant dispenser operated by one of those squirt pumps in the top. Jesus. Did she apply the stuff like sunscreen? The whole thing was incredibly tawdry. Angela flicked off the bathroom light and stood at the door, one hand resting high on the door jamb. 'Do you want to do it?' she asked cheekily. I wanted to do anything but. I wanted to walk downstairs with her, so I took her hand and led her out of the room and out the front door onto the street and away from that place, and as we locked the door I experienced a sense of overwhelming relief.

* * *

Kings Cross again, the next day. I was on my lunch break pocketing fifteen minutes of slow time in a park with an old homeless man who sat with me on a low wall, turning his cigarette to ash by breathing gently and patiently. He was a piece of thin wire stretched taut, lean and rangy. He would sleep rough that night. His cigarette burned to the nub and he tossed the fag end into the gutter like it had disappointed him. I munched my lunch. As we sat in the sun, sharing the same space but with a polite distance between us, we both noticed at the same time an albino walking down Macleay Street towards us. The old man and I watched him approach through the gentle swish of the passing traffic. He was eating a meat pie. He walked with a swagger. As he drew level with the old man he swallowed the last piece of crust, scrunched the paper bag into a tight ball and threw it into the old man's face. 'Fucking bum,' he scowled, and passed by, leaving my companion looking startled, hurt and bewildered. As the albino disappeared around a corner further down the street, the old man turned to me sadly, and shook his head. 'People are shits,' he observed regretfully.

*   *   *

I arranged for a counselling session with Mary and when the door was closed and we were alone I gently told her about my relationship with Angela. I couldn't lie to her after all that we had shared together. Five years. Besides, it had been one of our rules from the start. Outside of Faith, I was permitted no lovers. I abided by the rules. I had to end it with both Mary and Faith. Mary took the news quietly but I could see that I had hurt her. My own heart was aching. Mary leant forward in her chair and put her face in her hands. She sat with her knees together. She seemed so girlish and small, two words that I would never have thought to use of Mary at any other time. I knelt beside her chair and put my arms around her. She submitted to the embrace, leaning against me, sobbing softly into her hands. 'I'm sorry, Mary.' 'I should have left him for you.' 'I'm sorry.' 'I should have left him.' 'I'm sorry.' 'I have wasted you, Simon.' 'I'm sorry. I'm sorry. I'm sorry.'

*   *   *

Later, with her eyes still moist, Mary asked to see a photo of Angela. I went to my desk and took a digital camera out of the drawer. I moved to Mary's side and turned it on. I held it up so that Mary could see the screen. It was a photo of Angela taken two days before, her head and shoulders, just a face with a half-smile on it, taken when she wasn't expecting it. Mary drew in a deep breath and let it out with a sad sigh. 'Oh Simon,' she muttered sadly, 'she will hurt you.'

*   *   *

But Angela and I were going at it like porn-monkeys on ecstasy. In those first few weeks I couldn't stop myself. I gorged myself like a pig on her, shamelessly. My testicles ached. I picture them now as a pair of panting exhausted dogs, heads drooping, tongues lolling. I would only realise later that it was also making me selfish and that I was becoming a bore. And somewhere beneath the throbbing of my balls an ill-defined thought had started to eddy. Angela was beautiful, witty, sexy, intelligent, amusing, sincere, kind and quirky. Quite a combination. But when Mister Theory asked about 'this new sheila' the only adjective I used of the many was the one that started with q.

*   *   *

The last thing that Mary said to me when she left my office that day, in a commanding voice but a sisterly tone, was, 'Don't tell Faith yet. She wouldn't understand.' But I had not seen Faith to tell her anything. She had stopped attending church. She was not returning calls. Word finally came through to me that she and Hallum were on holidays. A postcard arrived from Florence. A picture of Michelangelo's David, his enormous hands and balls. *Enjoying the sights. Thinking of you.* Unsigned.

*   *   *

Looking back on it I think that it first started to unravel the day that Angela and I caught the ferry to Manly for a pleasant day by the sea. It was a clear morning. The sun was shining and the sky was blue, just as they are meant to be on such days. The temperature was perfect, warm at 10am with just a hint of a cooling breeze. We walked arm in arm along Circular Quay heading for our ferry. Waves swelled and lapped at the jetty piers. They sloshed against the sea wall with the passing water traffic. I had a beautiful woman on my arm. She was chattering away about something. It didn't matter what. She was very happy and I was vain enough to know that at least part of that was down to me. Me! Sure, the end of my knob throbbed with exhaustion but the results that morning had been entirely worth it. Angela was delighted with the world. And she was doing that thing, that thing that always undid me. In between her gabble and chatter she would look up into my face and smile. Looking to me (me!) for my smile, my nod, my witty one liners. Me!

We boarded the ferry and it edged out of Sydney Cove. We had taken seats on the starboard side so the Opera House slipped by as we headed into the harbour. Pleasure craft bobbed all around us. Angela was sitting as close to me as is humanly possible. I could feel the soft warmth of the flesh on her hip pressed against my own thigh and one of her hands gripped my biceps. A beautiful girl. A beautiful day. Throbbing bits. I was irredeemably happy. Right? Wrong. I was oddly on edge. By then I had seen my darling Angela perform astonishing acts in the bedroom but I realised then, on that ferry, that I had never really been out in public with her. In fact this was our first real outing, and frankly it takes much less to embarrass me in public than it does in the bedroom. And ironically it was precisely the thing that in the bedroom I loved that in public I was feeling uncomfortable about. Angela was an *incredibly* sexy woman. In bed, straddling my undeserving body, incredibly sexy was great, but on the ferry to Manly it was doing my head in. Men gawped at her. They stared at her breasts. I heard murmured comments as she walked past labourers eating hamburgers. Angela was clearly used to this. She was aware of it and gave the impression that she might have been ignoring it. But sometimes I detected the faintest blush when an indiscreet comment was made, and sometimes, to my irritation, maybe even a little return flirtatious glance, maybe even the hint of a smile, maybe. But for whose benefit? Nevertheless, mostly she ignored and ignored and carried on chirping away in my ear while I became more and more conscious of the fact that the men would look first at her and then at me, and in their eyes there was the judgement that I myself would have made: you don't deserve her. They couldn't have made it any more obvious if they'd tried. Their sneers. Their looks of derision.

And poor Angela. Is this what life was like for her? I was suddenly aware of the predators. Their eyes settled on her like vultures on carrion. Their looks resembled the alert-lazy gazes of lions. She moved from place to place like a wounded gazelle. Angela, the gazelle. She just kept grazing. Head down, for the most part, flanks twitching. There is power in beauty-flavoured vulnerability. And there is vulnerability in it too. And there was definitely something there. A jumpiness in her. The eye always looking out for danger. Skittish. And perhaps there was more than a little in the way of over-compensation. I turned to her and observed her clothing. A miniscule skirt, so short that she had to sit with her thighs clamped together to avoid flashing the whole of Sydney Harbour. And I knew for a fact what was going on down there. I had watched her dress that morning, pulling on her skimpy g-string underpants, poking her bottom out, bending a little forward, shaking her bum, and straightening up into them. One unexpected gust of sea breeze would expose a very pert and very bare bottom bisected by a g-string so narrow I wonder she didn't get a paper cut. And her t-shirt. So tight I could make out her nipples as the cool sea air began to exert itself. Me and every other bugger on the ferry. A man walked by holding his one-year-old child in his arms. As he passed he looked down on Angela, past his cooing child, and he very deliberately, very carefully, had a good long look at Angela's chest. Even the child gave them the once over with a professional and experienced eye. Angela ignored him. I felt a surge of protectiveness. I couldn't have felt any more affronted than if he'd actually paused, passed me his child, and given them a little rub.

I looked again at her short skirt and her tight t-shirt, and it started to creep into my brain like a toxin. It worried me that she wouldn't tone down the clothing a little; for her own sake, I told myself. In other words, I was beginning to blame her. And it was going to get worse, worse because I was weak and untrusting and awful. And worse because she bloody loved it, loved me bristling with jealousy, loved the raw power that her gawping admirers relinquished to her and her g-strung bum. This brandishing of her body, this refusal to let horrid men ruin her day and change her manner of living, this thing that I should have embraced as wonderful would take it all apart. Because it hurt me while it made her feel good, and it didn't seem to bother her that it hurt me. And the more she sensed my irritation, the more she'd push it, asserting her independence, demanding my loyalty and trust. Disaster written all over it.

And the first step in that direction involved a little patch of dry skin. Angela had been complaining of an itching all morning where her bra was rubbing. And there on the starboard side of the Manly ferry, with the clear blue sky and oglesome men, she lifted up her t-shirt, scooped the left breast out of its cup, lifted her left arm and asked if I could see anything. Could I fucking *see* anything?! 'I can see your fucking tit is what I can see,' I hissed, mortified, as I looked manically around the deck and tried to cover up the uncovered with my open hands. And I could see half a dozen men with their jaws gaping open, was what I could see. I could see the cheerful pink little nipple cringing in the bold sunlight. And I could see the look of hurt transitioning to quiet triumph in Angela's eye when I hastily pulled her shirt down and got all prudish and paternal with her. I realise now that she was making a statement. She was telling them all to fuck off, telling them all that they could look but never have what I had, and telling me to accept and trust, because she was who she was and she wasn't going to be quiet and ugly for anybody. But that's not the message that I got, and it was all downhill from there.

* * *

Every job gets boring. Even if it is something that you live for. Even if it's something that you love. I can't be sure but I suspect that even Mother Theresa walked into the Calcutta clinic once in a while and thought to herself, 'Oh Christ, not another leper!' So you can imagine how tough it got for me after I realised I didn't believe in God. It got very boring indeed. And challenging. Not least of all because I was not immune to the ironies or to my hypocrisy.

An example:

I am performing a wedding ceremony in the church of the Ministry of Christ, surrounded by friends and family of the bride and groom, all of whom seem to be hanging on my every mundane word. I have just delivered my spiel on fidelity, lying sincerely and fluently to the bride and groom from the altar, a look of studied piety on my face. A congregation of gazes fails to discern my two-facedness because everything that I say is said with a Bible in my hand, the most effective smoke-screen of them all. The bride is sweet. The groom is nice. For all my cynicism I really do wish them all the happiness in the world. But my good wishes are wasted. I know that. Any fool would. Today, the young couple will pledge themselves 'till death do us part' but I can already hear the clock ticking urgently in the background. One look at that bride, sweet and charming and witty and sensual, tells me that they don't stand a chance. Specifically, *he* doesn't stand a chance. Where he is nice and good and reliable, she is vivacious, bright and passionate. In fact, she is streets ahead in all the things that count, the attractive things, the things that men want to have sex with. She's marrying a plodder. Nice but dull. She is curious and flirtatious, keen to know the world. Most importantly, she has edge. She doesn't know it yet but in a few years time, this man will bore the tits off her. Nevertheless, for now she gazes into his eyes with unadulterated adoration, and he returns her looks with a red blush to his pimply cheeks. First meets first, blind to a world of opportunity. It's all very endearing but even as I remind them of the importance of their vows my eyes have settled on the flawless skin of the bride's throat and chest and I am picturing her welcoming me to her bed with beckoning hands and loosening thighs, five years from now, 2.15pm, when husbands are at work, blithe and oblivious. It sounds cruel but it would be a kindness. Five years from now she will be miserable.

The Ministry of Christ was a 'love, honour and obey' church. God demanded obedience. Husbands demanded it also, even the pimply blushing ones in slightly ill-fitting tuxes, with thin pale wrists poking out the ends of over-short cuffs. It was also the kind of church that valued virginity because it said that the person had done as they were told well into their post-pubescent years. Virginity would be taken. Taken. The church and its obsession with virgins, as if a woman that has made love is somehow diminished by the experience.

I remember that we worked our way through the vows, the happy couple obediently repeating the words after me, and as each one spoke I recall that I had eyes only for the bride. Pure and virginal. I smiled encouragingly at her through her vows and allowed wicked thoughts to flit through my imagination. Not that I ever would have done anything with her. I had no desire to corrupt the woman. However, I would have liked to have made love with her eventually, just not then. I wouldn't want to take her virginity. I'd want no clumsiness, shyness or pain in her experience. No. I'd rather be the *second*. I'd rather wait the five years, share her bed when she had solved for herself some of the mysteries in sex, when the flesh and fluids of the act excited without embarrassment, when she had refined her tastes and knew her wants, approaching sex hungrily and unashamedly, with confident caresses, giving and taking in equal measure, consenting. And when she had learned that the exchange has *nothing* to do with obeying.

* * *

One morning Angela told me that she hated her bum. She spoke of it like it was something in another room, not really part of her, a burden that she had to cart around in her shoulder bag. When I asked why, she pouted and complained that she could feel it wobble when she walked. I was lying in bed. I watched her kick off the blankets, stand up and walk huffily from our bed to the bathroom, naked. Frankly, I *was* amazed by how much of her body moved when she moved. Her breasts, her thighs and bottom. Amazed and aroused. I can't help but think that she had used the wrong word entirely. Not wobble. Quiver.

* * *

Another Sunday morning service. I arrived early, as always, and helped to put out the chairs while Gregory moved about the hall watering the pot plants that lined the walls. The band was setting up while we went about our work, thumping drums and sound-checking. Angela was in bed back at her place where I had left her about an hour before, mouth-breathing in her sleep, tangled in the sheets that she had a tendency to appropriate. It was all too weird. In a little over an hour I would deliver a sermon on Paul's letter to the Ephesians. Sometimes my own hypocrisy dazzled me. As I lugged tall stacks of chairs across the church hall Caroline with the bucked teeth started her vocal exercises, warming up for the singing that would come later in the morning. After a minute or two of exercises she dropped subtly into 'Amazing Grace'. Her voice was a clear feminine one, beautiful but understated. *Amazing Grace how sweet the sound*. I paused, resting the pile of chairs on the ground. *That saved a wretch like me*. In this hall, in the hour before my sermon, my girlfriend at home in a bed that smelled of our bodies, I felt a wave of sudden emotion. It wasn't shame but it drew water from there. It was not that *my* world was so fucked up. It was that *the* world was so fucked up. I was a Minister of Religion who married people, counselled people, healed people and in my down time slept with someone in the sex industry. And you know what? It was not even all that unusual! But it was turning me into something that I was beginning to hate. I didn't want to hurt anybody but I knew that that was the only way that it could all end. *I once was lost but now am found*. These people could be so fucking nice. I couldn't bear it any more. Suddenly Gregory was standing by my side. 'Are you alright?' he asked, resting his hand on my shoulder. I nodded. He smiled and returned to watering the plants. And me? Wretched.

*   *   *

After the service I caught Patti and Pru as they were making for the door. They both gave me a big hug and Patti squeezed my cheeks like I was five years old. Pru looked very thin although better than she had looked the last time I had seen her. Patti seemed distracted, supporting Pru with one arm as they stood in front of me. With some reticence I asked how Pru's health was.

She waved the question away. 'The doctors have given me the all clear,' she declared with frustration. 'Can you believe the whole palaver was a false alarm!'

* * *

I ran into Mary and Donald in the car park. I shook Donald's hand and pecked Mary on the cheek. Her scent filled my nostrils and I felt all the strength in my body turn to something as light as pollen. I could have floated away. Was it still love? Even now? We chatted politely for a couple of minutes and I casually made the observation that it had been quite some time since we had last had a counselling session. Donald half-shrugged as if he was surprised himself and told me that they hadn't really felt the need for it lately. Things just seemed to have improved between them, he said. I felt the blood drain from my face. Mary didn't meet my eye, she toed the ground with her foot. It was all too much. Donald touched Mary's shoulder fondly, and to my astonishment I felt tears come to my eyes. My mouth ran dry. Was it jealousy I was feeling? Surely not. Guilt? After all this time? Maybe. No. I knew what it was. I had failed her. For five long years, I had failed her and her husband and daughter. Who would have thought it! I was an arsehole after all! I drew a quick deep breath and turned away from them both, finding a reason to end the conversation and move quickly into the church. As I turned to leave I sensed Mary glance up at me briefly but I dared not look at her for fear of what I might see in her face. Hate? Anger? Resentment? Oh, what could save a wretch like me?

* * *

Angela could. Some powerful magic was at work. Black magic. I couldn't stop thinking about her. Couldn't take my eyes off her. Couldn't stop touching her. But it wasn't all beer and skittles. There was, for example, the Sociology Ball which was another distinct stage in the death of our relationship. It all started well enough with me lying on my back in bed, hands behind my head,

110

watching Angela move busily about the room in her underwear, preparing for our first big night out together. My eyes followed her as she went about her getting-ready business, ironing her clothes, bending over the ironing board intently, pressing down on the iron. Ironing done, I watched her as she took a seat in front of the mirror and absently teased out her long dark hair with a brush, head tilted sideways against the strokes. Not growing bored for an instant, I watched her as she leant her face to the mirror, applying lipstick, eyeliner, foundation. I watched her pucker her lips for the lipstick, roll her eyes for the eyeliner, point her chin for the foundation. I took in the whole show as if it were performed for me. I couldn't help it. Angela seemed so happy, humming snatches of song between applications of make-up, clacking lids back onto jars of goop officiously, unzipping and rezipping cosmetics cases. I was experiencing the most potent brand of affection, where the happiness of the woman I was with was enough to bring me happiness, and where in fact my own happiness was secondary to hers. I would have done just about anything that night to ensure that Angela stayed that way. If I could, I would have shielded her from the world's cruelties forever.

Finally, show almost over, Angela left the room for a few minutes, emerging from the bathroom, still in her undies, looking beautiful. She spied me watching her and frowned. 'You should get dressed or we'll be late,' she scolded but I lay there for another two minutes watching her step into her gown. Angela drew it up over her body, smoothing the fabric over her bottom and hips, settling it across her body with her hands. When she had finished she stood in front of the mirror and appraised herself from all angles. 'How do I look?' she asked, looking like she wasn't going to like the answer. I rose from the bed and went to her. For an answer, I kissed her throat.

It took a lot of begging but I had been suborned by Professor Martin to attend the Sociology Ball, a debauched event organised annually by a society of sociology students from the university. The thought of attending the ball left me cold but when I told Angela she jumped out of her chair like an eight year old, clapped her hands excitedly and yelled, 'Goodie!' 'It'll be fun,' she insisted, but I had long had my doubts. Angela suggested that at the ball we would tell everyone that we were just friends because she was worried that the other students would get jealous if they knew we were having an affair. For my part, I accepted her suggestion with some relief, and the relief with a sense of guilt. Why relief? Because I was still hiding things, Angela, from my world, and yet, leaving the house together that night, I felt a surge of pride. This magnificent, beautiful woman was my girlfriend! I could hardly wipe the smile off my face.

The Sociology Ball was held in an old school hall near the university. When Angela and I arrived, the timber walls and floor were trembling with thumping music and the palpitating sex glands of about two hundred undergrads. The room was heaving with it. We entered the hall, our progress followed by about a hundred sets of covetous male eyes. Angela floated across the floor, resting her hand in the bend of my arm, and I experienced another surge of pride. I was the envy of every man in the room. We found a place for ourselves in one corner and I revelled in my new situation. Angela stood very close to me. I could feel her warm body pressed against my side. It was going to be hard to pretend that we were just friends afterwards but I don't think I cared anymore. I wanted to dance with her, hold her, kiss her, there, in front of everybody. Fuck the church and fuck anybody else that is interested, I was thinking. I looked around the room. Clusters of resentful twenty-one-year-old men were forming. They talked amongst themselves, beers in hands, occasionally looking sullenly in my direction as if they were co-ordinating a Mafia hit. The music pumped away, and as the boys plotted my murder, they jived their heads slightly to its rhythms, their eyes cold in spite of the upbeat tempo. Jealousy. Fuck them. Let them stew.

I heard Angela say something into my ear but I couldn't quite make it out above the music. Before I could reply she had left my side. I turned and watched her disappear in the direction of the bar. I found myself standing to one side of a dance floor, hands in my pockets, watching a clutch of young women dancing around their handbags. The lights were low. Mirror balls and flashing lights provided a little illumination but there were many dark corners for naughty youthful kissing later in the evening. I watched a few girls in lurid evening gowns stagger between groups of men, trying to entice them with drunken cleavage. The socially inadequate men watched the ones that could dance with a look of undisguised contempt. I looked around for Angela. Now where had she gone?

I made my way through the milling crowd, past the dancers, past the throbbing music speakers, searching for Angela. I was still feeling great. Angela had made me feel like the king of the world. Had she any idea of the power she wielded? These thoughts and feelings were swirling through my mind when I spied her across the room chatting to a group of young male students. I watched her in mounting confusion and surprise, my heart sinking. She had turned into another human being. Ten minutes before she had been Grace Kelly circa 1955, now she was Veronica the Talent circa 2am. Angela was flirting with one of the men outrageously. She laughed and touched his forearm, she half-tripped half-fell into him, allowed herself to be righted with a firm hand on her waist, allowed the hand to wander, didn't stop it when it brushed her backside. She fluttered her eyelashes at him, she smiled and giggled. She played the part of the sexy little innocent. He had her undivided attention. And all the while, she was breaking my heart. My mouth dry, my face burning, I walked away. I couldn't bear it. Was I weak? I bought a drink and returned to my corner. For the next twenty minutes I sipped warm flat beer from a plastic cup, watching Angela on the dance floor with her new friend. I watched her hips grind and sway, her eyes closed, feeling the music. I felt worthless. Finally she disengaged from the man and ran over to me breathlessly. She was laughing when she reached me. She snatched the beer from my hand and took a swig. I could hardly bring myself to speak. I felt hurt and betrayed, but Angela laughed at me. 'What's gotten into you?' I didn't reply. I sipped my beer in silent resentment. Angela turned briefly to look at the man she had been dancing with. He was looking in my direction with slaughter in his eye. 'God, Simon, you're not jealous of him are you?' Angela said incredulously. 'He's just a boy!' Again I said nothing. She was making me feel stupid. Angela stood on her tip-toes, throwing one arm around my neck. She aggressively pulled my head forward so that my face was tilted towards hers. She planted a long warm kiss on my mouth that must have been agony for the other bloke to witness. 'He's a dickhead,' she said dismissively when the kiss had come to an end, and by the look in her eye it was clear that he never really mattered. In fact, of the two of us, I was the only one that seemed to care about his feelings.

*   *   *

Two nights later I was at home alone in the early evening. The house was a silent frame for me sitting slumped in the lounge room in my armchair, absorbing the stillness, my mind in a kind of neutral condition but inclining inexplicably towards maudlin. I should have been happy. But my life still seemed to be tilting on a new axis, one I had no control over. Then the telephone rang. I rose with creaking knees and answered it. I heard Faith on the other end of the line, her voice hollow with the distance between us. She cried 'Simon!' when I answered, and I felt my heart lift. It was a voice from my old axis, cheerful but also laced with something that wasn't cheerful. Before I could reply she said, 'Greetings from Edinburgh,' and laughed a little nervously. We fell to talking immediately. We were old lovers and old friends again.

Faith told me that Hallum had taken up a secondment with the British office. She talked about the mechanical engineering world where Hallum was a mover and shaker. Car parts. Something. I was not taking it in. All I could hear was the familiar timbre and lilt in her voice, the soft laughter between sentences, her rush to speak the words she had been saving up over the last few weeks. We were like two teenagers babbling and gabbling over the top of each other. I asked when she'd be coming home and was met with a sudden seriousness. 'Not for a while,' she replied. 'The secondment is for two years.'

I could hear Faith breathing on the other end of the line. A hemisphere away. She ended the silence for me. 'I'm sorry, Simon. I should have come to say good-bye. But right up until I got on the plane I never thought I'd do it. I told myself I'd leave him. I had made up my mind to leave him. But I was just too scared in the end, Simon. I guess I just …' Her voice trailed off. After a second or two she finished her sentence. 'I chickened out,' she murmured. Then, again, 'I'm sorry.' There was a pause as we both felt for our words. Faith broke the silence, 'Do you miss me, Simon?'

'Of course. Of course.' I didn't mention Angela. There seemed no point.

'Simon, I wanted to call to say a proper good-bye.'

'I'm glad you called, Faith. I am.'

'And I wanted to thank you.'

'Me? What for?'

'For being kind to me.'

'Oh Faith.'

'No, Simon. I mean it. You made me feel valued.'

I didn't know what to say. If the truth's to be told I had always feared that I was just messing things up for Faith, complicating things with a bunch of questions, and leaving her after each encounter with fewer and fewer answers. I wanted to tell her that. I wanted her to know how scared I was of hurting her. Instead, it was Faith again who spoke first. 'You were *good* for me.' I couldn't think of any words to say. When I said, 'I miss you, Faith,' it hardly seemed enough but I could tell that Faith was moved by the tone in my voice. We had performed a range of sex acts breath-taking in their scope and variety and only then could we find it in ourselves to feel embarrassed, by words.

We steered the conversation to safer territory. Edinburgh. The tourist sites. Her new home. We were enjoying the conversation when Faith suddenly halted mid-sentence and groaned, 'Oh no! It's my husband. He's just pulled into the drive.' She sounded distressed and I tried to reassure her but Faith told me it was awful timing. She had other news for me. Big news. Important news. She spoke quickly, 'I'll call again, Simon. I will.

115

Maybe not straight away though. I need to think about some things.' It was all sounding very mysterious but I didn't pursue it. 'Don't worry, Faith. It's alright,' I reassured her. Faith said quietly, 'I want you to be happy.'

'I'll try.'

'I mean it, Simon. I wasn't the only unhappy one in our bed.'

'Good-bye, Faith.'

'Good-bye.' I was about to hang up when I heard Faith again.

'Simon?'

'Yes, Faith.'

'We never did anything that I am ashamed of.'

She hung up, and I did the same. In my mind I could see Hallum walking in the door and Faith turning to greet him, consenting to a peck on the cheek, blinking the memories of me away as Hallum left the room again. Half an hour later I was still sitting in the same silent lounge room, the same slump in the same lounge chair. I heard the key in the front door and Angela pushed the door open, walked into the hall, and dumped a bag of library books onto the floor boards. She walked into the lounge room cheerfully. We exchanged hi's. I didn't get up but tilted my head in readiness for the kiss. She crossed the room and planted one on me, then turned to ease her bottom onto my lap, swinging her knees over the armrest so that she was in profile to me. I looped my arms around her waist and kissed her cheek. She kissed me back. 'How was your day?' she asked. I told her it was okay. 'Just okay?' she teased, poking out her bottom lip in sympathy. 'I've had better,' I said.

* * *

'I worry sometimes that I might hurt you,' I said softly. Angela raised her head from her pillow to look at my face. 'Are you going to do something mean?' she asked with a touch of concern. She thought I meant hurt her emotionally. I was surprised to see something like fear creep into her expression. I put my arms around her body and held her tenderly. I explained soothingly that with all this sex I was worried that I'd hurt her 'down there', and to further demonstrate my facility with the English language I clarified with 'between the legs'. She laughed. 'Don't be silly,' she chided. 'I'll tell you if it hurts!' Then to really make me feel better she told me that my dick fitted her perfectly. The wrong size, apparently, can be really uncomfortable. Then Steve got a look-in. Steve was her ex-boyfriend. Steve was rarely spoken about. I never asked and she never volunteered any information but when his name came up from time to time there was always a sense that he had hurt her badly. Little did I know! Angela educated me. 'Steve was awful,' she said with pursed lips. 'Rough?' I asked stupidly. 'Oh no!' she corrected me. 'He had a *really* big one.' Well that's just. Fucking. Terrific. With Angela lying there next to me with what might have been a faint smile on her face while she reminisced, I sought some positive reinforcement. 'So you're sure mine fits okay then?' I asked, not quite managing to avoid sounding a little plaintive. She confirmed very seriously that it was a perfect fit. Then suddenly all smiley and reassuring she said she wouldn't change it if she could. Then serious again, 'I don't like the really big ones.' I lay back beside her and stared at the ceiling. Now who's worried about pitching hotdogs down corridors?

I disliked Steve. Angela had shown me her photo album. A catalogue of photos recording in chronological order their seven years together. His big masculine jaw. His big white teeth. His big dopey crooked but strangely attractive grin. His deep suntan and sun-bleached hair. He was usually smiling into the camera clad in sporting attire or with the accoutrements of physical achievement under his arm. Wetsuit. Rugby jersey. Gym gear. Surf board. He was fit and muscular and broad shouldered. He had the Australian outdoors look. He looked like he could be relied on in a fight, but he also looked like he might *start* the fight. There was a look in his eye, behind his eyes, a set to his jaw, a slight sneer of the top lip, that said he'd be up for just about anything and that if it all went bad he'd be at the heart of it. Even in his photos Steve looked a little menacing.

Angela was nineteen when she met Steve. The early photos showed her a very young nineteen, cute rather than beautiful. In every photo she was under Steve's arm. He was a few years older and in most of the pictures he would hold her roughly. She was invariably squeezed against his side, looking at the camera from within a body twisted by his bicepped arm. She looked determined, not happy. It could be he was being protective but it could have been more. Angela usually looked uncertain of herself in these pictures, but also clearly keen on Steve. The camera often caught her looking up into his face adoringly. These photos made me jealous. In my world she had invented that look for me. More photos later showed Angela developing her own personality. Photos of her with friends other than Steve. Young women in bars, around pools, on picnics. In these photos Angela was smiling. She looked incredible. The camera loved her. It loved her big dark eyes. Looking at her photos I began to realise that I might too. Love. And then the shot of Steve shirtless on the lounge chair, pecs glistening and brown, board shorts and bare feet, his eyes closed in ecstasy as he sucked on an enormous spliff. Looking into the camera in the next photo his unfocussed eyes stared me down. Wreathed in sweet dope smoke he looked *my* way, and at Angela behind the camera, and I didn't like what I saw. His look said, 'Fuck you,' and I could see why she might have been afraid of him.

'I don't think I want to hear any more about Steve and his amazing technicolour dream penis,' I told Angela. She realised now that she had made me feel bad. She pinched me so hard it hurt and laughed when I shrank away from her. 'Don't worry about Steve,' she told me, suddenly serious. 'Steve was a fucking idiot.'

* * *

More magic:
I close The Mission one evening and turn to wave to Angela who stands on the other side of the street. She moves to the kerb and looks both ways, preparing to run across to me. I feel

118

a sudden wave of panic. I want to cry out 'be careful darling' but she looks controlled and self-assured, waiting for a gap in the traffic. When one appears she trots from one kerb to the other with a womanish run, elbows at her waist, knees low and together, hands out-balanced, which surprises me given her bedroom athleticism. I follow her progress with an affectionate smile. Mid-run, she glances up and sees me watching her, blushes, and crosses the second half of the street in a state of hyper self-awareness. Poor Angela leaves the far kerb a confident chin-held-high woman and arrives at mine a blushing, eye-averting girl. I open my arms to her and she buries her face into my jumper with endearing embarrassment. I hold her to me and suck the scent into my nostrils like a dog.

Self-conscious. And yet. Later that night Angela and I engage in some nude wrestling that ends with her sitting on my belly and pinning my arms above my head by the wrists. I concede to it, both of us laughing, Angela pulling herself together long enough to narrow her eyes in an effort to look tough, but squealing and bursting out laughing again when I almost buck her off me. She has to arch her back to reach my wrists. Her boobs dangle at my chin. Her laughter subsides into panting. She eases her bum back and kisses my mouth then rises onto her knees and wriggles forward. Reaching between her legs she draws back the bow-tip of her labia, exposing the pale clitoris, and lowers herself onto my mouth. It's been a cold evening and the moist outer lips feel cool at first, but there's warmth at the heart and my tongue probes the opening to her body for it. My last vision of Angela is of her closing her eyes and tilting her head back. Not self-conscious. Not self-conscious at all.

*   *   *

But it was around this time that I started to feel a little ashamed of myself. I had been spending less and less time at The Mission, preferring instead the company of Angela, and yet it was The Mission that provided something of a justification for my Sunday School hypocrisies. Without it, I was simply a liar. So I forced myself to spend a full week in the Cross, including the night shifts, experiencing my old world in a distracted way. Angela dropped by briefly each evening on her way to Zanadu, dressed to the nines, short skirts and breasty-nipply tops, but usually I was alone with my thoughts and the occasional drug-addled, drunk, desperate or scared prostitute.

On one Friday evening I sat quietly in The Mission window next to our Christian magazine rack and watched the tangle of Kings Cross tease out now and then into the individual characters and visions that make a city. Snatches of conversation, laughter, shrieks and shouts filtered into The Mission where the tick and erratic blink of a dodgy fluorescent light seemed to capture my mood exactly. I sat quietly and stared as the evening turned to night, leaving me illuminated in my cube of stuttering white light. A noise at the window brought me back to the world. It was Evie tapping on the pane with her long synthetic nails. Our eyes met and she pulled a silly face. She walked in sassily and tossed me my chocolate bar. 'Hey preacher!' she said and laughed at nothing.

Evie was in a great mood that night, on her way to work. She told me she had made a fortune the previous Monday night when a Japanese industry group was in town. 'Eight in a row!' she told me shamelessly, 'And not one of them lasted more than six minutes!' She laughed loudly, and laughed even more when she saw my disapproving look. We chatted for a while, and just as Evie was about to leave, Angela walked in, also on her way to work. Evie said, 'Hi,' a little uncertainly but cheerily enough, and Angela returned the greeting, then she walked over to me and kissed me briefly on the mouth. Evie could barely contain her astonishment. Her eyes opened wide, her jaw dropped. As Angela's lips and mine parted company there was a horrible pregnant nothingness that lasted about a year until Evie broke the silence with, 'I do *not* believe it!' I said nothing. Evie waggled a finger at me and said, 'You naughty *naughty* boy.' Angela and Evie burst out laughing, revelling in my mortification but this was a watershed moment. Finally I said to Evie, 'This is Angela. A friend.' The last word was pathetically weak and Angela registered it with a slight shift of her eyebrows. We chatted and I clumsily explained things but Evie was still shaking her head five minutes later when she reluctantly left for the brothel. When we were alone, Angela gave me an ambiguous look. I felt like a terrible heel. Over the last few weeks Angela had, with *incredible* equanimity, allowed me to perform some of the most creative sex acts that I could dream up, and the best I could do was call her 'a friend'. I stood before her cringing internally. I knew it. I was an arsehole.

It's not like I ever decided that I wanted to keep her a secret. She couldn't say I hadn't taken her to places, to movies, to restaurants, but I have to admit that I had always done so with a certain self-consciousness and the nagging fear that I'd be spotted by one of my flock of stone-casting Old Testamenters. And if that happened, I knew I was fucked. In fact, Angela and I had never really discussed my double life at all. Of course, Angela knew plenty about it. My CV was widely advertised when I started lecturing at the university, and she had asked a few questions, but she was remarkably uninterested, and very far from being critical of what most people would consider to be blatant and ridiculous bullshit. But Angela was accustomed to the schizophrenic existence of the prostitutes that she worked with, the separation of body and soul that that entails, and seemed unaffected by my own alter ego. To tell the truth, I think she rather liked it. Certainly Sunday evening sex always seemed to bring out the best in her. But seeing me at The Mission, she must have been beginning to understand that she did not fit somehow, and that could only offend and hurt her.

And then, with impeccable timing, Gregory walked into The Mission, Bible in one hand, all 'Bless you, brother' and 'Hallelujah'. He shook my hand with a dopey evangelical grin on his face and turned to Angela with a 'Praise the Lord'. She shook his hand, all the while looking at *me*. 'And who might you be, sister?' Gregory asked. My heart rate accelerated to phenomenal levels. I saw my life going out the window but, as it turned out, I had nothing to fear. My angelic Angela was no fool. She knew how to play this game better than any of us. She introduced herself as 'Angela ... a friend' and made to leave. As she did so, big blundering Gregory asked which 'establishment' she worked in. He had assumed she was a prostitute. It infuriated and horrified me, but later I recalled with shame that I had once done the same thing. Angela told him coolly she was on reception at Zanadu. Gregory received the news with a regretful shaking of the head but Angela dealt him a withering glare which pulled even Gregory up short, then she asked him where he bought his shoes. He looked surprised then a little proud and told her. She received the news with her own regretful shaking of the head, leaving Gregory looking utterly destroyed. Then Angela waved me good-bye with a little smile, turned and hip-swinged out the door. Gregory experienced her departure as if she'd just been posted to Stalingrad 1943, but then glanced at his shoes confusedly. I was actually sneaking a peek at Angela's bum when Gregory turned his attention back to me. He caught me smiling and frowned, then got his revenge by ruining the next hour of my life by sitting with me and chatting companionably.

Later that night, at 2am, as I pulled down the security grille on The Mission and began locking up, Angela approached me. It was knock-off time for her as well. She kissed my mouth, one arm crooked around my neck. When we disengaged she said firmly but not unkindly, 'I let you off once today. I will let you off twice. And maybe even a third and a fourth time. But one day, at a time of my choosing, I will not allow it any more. I am *not* something to be ashamed of.' She kissed me again. I apologised. She accepted the apology graciously. I went home with her and wondered at the depth of her good grace and her patience with my dirty little secrets.

* * *

Memory:

Angela is in my bed, as she has been for two days, with tonsillitis. She lies there in the late morning looking miserable. I sit on the edge of the mattress and she rolls over with theatrical sighing and a soft cough into her cupped hand. She really does look pathetic. I rest my hand on her shoulder and stroke the warm flesh. Angela closes her eyes and begins to nod off to sleep as my fingers brush the skin of her upper arm. Stroke, stroke, stroke. A slow gentle rhythm. We are connecting at the purest and most basic level. I smooth her hair. There is one thing that the church has gotten absolutely right. Touch and healing. The laying on of hands.

* * *

Angela is being mean again, although she seems oblivious to it. This time, it is the handsome young man in the dress shop that she is flirting with outrageously while I suffer and fume silently by the handbag rack. Angela plays all of the usual cards adeptly and shamelessly. The innocent little girl act. The accidentally-on-purpose over-balancing, coming to a stop with a bump of boob against body. The hand on his forearm. The giggles and eye flutters. I watch it all from the other side of the shop with a mix of anger and disappointment. It only makes it harder that she knows I am watching. I feel real pain. Every time that she does this stuff it demeans me, betrays me, hurts me. But today all of her tricks seem to be failing her. The man is totally unresponsive, if anything he's a little disdainful. Angela's flirtation could not be more obvious. Finally, with a hint of derision, the man rebuffs her with the comment that he's gay. His disclosure is met with relief. 'Thank God,' Angela says. 'I was beginning to think that there was something wrong with me.'

* * *

Angela was a welcome distraction, but I was really beginning to lose touch with how things were going at The Mission. Two weeks had passed before I even realised that Mister Theory was in trouble. This is how it went. One afternoon three men swaggered into Cherry Pop. They walked to the bar and asked to speak to the owner. The girl at the bar knew better than to get involved. The men looked mean. Gym monkeys. She could tell from the over-muscled shoulders and thick necks straining their collared shirts. She got Mister Theory who walked out casually from the back rooms. Mister Theory was no-one to mess with either but he'd never be a real thug, not like those guys. He was too trusting, too quick to laugh. He was smiling when he introduced himself and asked what he could do for them. Without speaking, one of the men struck Mister Theory hard across the face with an open hand. The slap of his palm against Mister Theory's cheek sounded like a rifle shot. There was a sudden silence, the horror that humans feel when confronted with unexpected violence. Mister Theory reeled but he was a tough customer. He returned to the upright and stared them down. Calmly, coolly, each syllable clearly enunciated, he said, 'Who the fuck are you?' The first man replied, 'We work for Mr Cekalovic. He says you owe him fifteen hundred dollars. We'll be back for it on Friday.' And with that, they turned and left.

Later, Mister Theory explained it for me. Cekalovic was new in town. He had just opened a brothel in Surry Hills. A dozen girls worked the rooms. It was a big investment. Cekalovic was looking to make a name for himself and he needed money so he sent his thugs into a bunch of brothels and bars in Kings Cross and started demanding money. It was that simple. He just demanded it. You paid him or you got hurt. There are men in the world who would think nothing of breaking the bones of another human being in order to pay off a mortgage.

But Mister Theory was no pussy. I asked him what he was going to do and he looked weary rather than scared. I looked at his hands. There were scars on his knuckles. He'd earned a reputation of his own. He told me matter-of-factly, 'First, I'm gunna fuck him. Then I'm gunna to go to the police.' I didn't doubt it for a second but this was a dangerous game and I was way out of my depth. I asked a sincere question. 'Do you think the cops will help?' Mister Theory looked very confident when he replied, 'They will if I pay them enough.'

* * *

124

Angela was telling me with some irritation to 'Hurry up and put it in'. I was kneeling behind her, naked, with a hesitant erection. She was on her hands and knees, bottom poised and quivering. From my enviable vantage point I could see two things: on the one hand, her gregarious vagina, a friendly lop-sided grin leering up at me from the shadow between her thighs, and on the other hand, as a kind of counterpoint, I could see her prudish anus nestled primly between her buttocks. The thing that Angela was encouraging me to 'hurry up and put it in' was the smaller of the two holes. She didn't get the response she was expecting. Exasperated, Angela turned around and faced me. We were both sitting on our heels, like two kids in a sandpit. She looked at me as if I was *the* biggest weirdo on the planet and shrugging, palms up, she demanded, 'What?'

'It's not really my thing,' I explained. Angela was having none of that. That was not the point, you see. She explained one more time that she wanted to give me a sex-present and that every man should *do* it just once so they can say they *have*. I told her I didn't want to. She told me exasperatedly that *that* didn't matter. I should do it anyway so that I *have* done it, she told me. 'But what about you?' I asked her. 'Do you enjoy it?' She shook her head and screwed up her nose. 'Yuk,' she said. Of course, I was completely confused. She read it in my eyes and flagging erection. She sighed and explained it for me one more time, like I was a thicky. She wanted to be the one that I *did* do it with, even if it *was* just once, and even if I *didn't* enjoy it. She wanted me to be able to say that I had done it, and when I said that, she wanted me to be thinking of *her*.

She turned around and presented her bottom again like a female chimp in oestrus. I glimpsed her reflection in the mirror on the other side of the room. Going by her facial expression she could have been waiting for a bus. And from me, no response. She turned, faced me again, sat on her heels. 'What?' she said but less demanding this time. I shook my head. I just didn't want to. I couldn't bear the thought of causing her pain or discomfort. I wanted her to feel only bliss when she was with me. I didn't want her grimacing. I didn't want her hurting. I just wanted her to have that eyes-closed-breathing-through-the-mouth-ecstasy-thing going on all the time when she was with me.

So I told her honestly, if she wanted to give me a special sex-present she should just give me a big wet kiss on the mouth. She didn't look all that convinced at first, but I must have had a sincere look about me because she relented, leant forward and pressed her mouth to mine. It was a warm lingering kiss. When we separated she held my limp bottom lip between her lips. She continued to hold it as she pulled away, stretching it then releasing it. It sprung back into place against my lower teeth with a slap. She laughed at me and we hugged. She had just given me something to cherish. She had given me one great image to carry around with me for the rest of my days: that poised bottom and the quiver.

We knew each other rather well by then. I had licked, smacked, kissed, wobbled, moistened, parted, stretched, tickled, strummed, rubbed and bounced the lot. I knew what things gave her goose bumps. And if I was ever in any doubt, she would clarify things for me with explicit and patient instructions. I was a dedicated student. I was a fast learner. But we were making the mistake of getting to know each other by body only. We were making the mistake of believing that because we didn't get embarrassed when errant semen lodged in her fringe we were getting close to each other. In fact, I knew what she looked like when she was happy. But that's all that I knew. Outside of her body, I didn't know what made her happy at all.

In fact, we didn't do much talking. We enjoyed talking, we just didn't do that much of it. Certainly, the post-coital conversations were nice. Long, lazy discussions that trickled into the night, but they didn't count for anything much, and I sometimes didn't even register what she was really saying. I just enjoyed the sound of her, the songs of her speech and its womanly intonations. After the cum-in-the-fringe episode I'm not sure that I would have even noticed if she had been lying there telling me about *Mein Kampf* and her favourite death camps. The conversations that really count take place in the local Woolworths next to the bargain bins. Sure, I'd been offered a go at her anus but had she ever asked me where I stand on the subject of meat after the use-by date has expired?

And her offer troubled me. It troubled me that she could divorce herself so completely from a part of her body (head up this end, bum down that end). It troubled me that she could give me access to it without expecting to derive any pleasure from it herself. Worse, without caring at all. Did that ever happen when we had 'normal' sex? And it troubled me that she would think that I'd derive pleasure out of seeing her grit her teeth in pain (simulated or otherwise) as I penetrated her. I just didn't see the fun in it, yet she had formed the view that I was the sort of person that might. It rankled.

The sentimental kissing and hugging over and done with, Angela turned back around and presented the other hole for my delectation. Looking back over her shoulder she asked, 'Will this do then?' 'Cheeky girl,' I scolded and lightly slapped her gorgeous arse. Then, after initiating the more conventional of the sex acts, I paused again mid-thrust as a thought occurred to me. I asked. 'So did Steve ever do it in your bum then?' I enquired with more than a little trepidation. Angela's reply sounded a bit nasal. Her forehead was resting on the bedsheets and the blood must have been going to her head. 'Oh no!' she replied matter-of-factly from under a headful of mussed-up hair. 'We tried but he was too big.' I got my rhythm back gradually, eyeing the *smaller* of the two holes again with renewed and miffed interest. Maybe a little discomfort wouldn't do her any harm, I thought.

*   *   *

This is how Mister Theory fucked Mr Cekalovic: he just let the girls in the industry know what was going on and left the rest to them. It was the beta-alpha male syndrome in operation. The next night, all twelve of Cekalovic's girls called in sick. The same again the following night. He was haemorrhaging money. He knew he was being screwed but didn't know by whom. He was ready to lash out but didn't know who to throw the first punch at. Then one afternoon he was pulled over in his BMW by an unmarked police car and the officers found a bag of cocaine in the glove compartment. It was that simple. Cekalovic knew a stitch-up when he saw one. He said nothing though he seethed silently beside the cops as they cuffed him. But Mister Theory was starting to look anxious. He knew he was in serious trouble if someone let the cat out of the bag.

*   *   *

Angela met me at The Mission one evening at closing time and we strolled together to the bus stop after I had locked up. Angela looked tired. She looped her arm through mine as we walked and talked quietly about her day. She was adorable. Her weariness made her seem vulnerable; there was a strangely attractive sensitiveness to her that night, almost childlike without being childish. Her body felt warm next to mine, our upper arms pressed together, hips brushing as we walked. We passed bars, cafés and restaurants full of people in spite of the late hour. We paid little attention to the hubbub. I didn't even notice the five men standing on the footpath outside the pub near the bus stop until one of them sneered, 'Hey bitch. How about a head job?' I interrupted my stride for an instant but didn't stop. The five men laughed amongst themselves, a deep, ugly, masculine sound, intimidating and provocative. 'Hey bitch,' he yelled, 'I'm talking to you.' This time I stopped. Angela pulled my arm and told me to leave it alone. There was a pleading tone in her voice. I held the man's stare. He grabbed his groin and thrust it in Angela's direction. 'Suck this,' he said. Then to me, his tone darkening, middle finger raised, 'Fuck you, buddy.' His mates started to laugh but the man continued to stare at me aggressively. There was no point in it. I let Angela pull me away and we headed for the bus stop again, gibes ringing in our ears. Angela was quiet on the bus back to my place. I tried to make conversation but she didn't have much to say. She responded in short sentences, with a soft voice. I made her a cup of tea when we got home and sat with her through the evening, the television for company, then Angela kissed me good-night and walked into the bedroom. I followed a few minutes later to find her curled up asleep on the bed.

I replayed the incident in my mind. Angela normally had a pretty thick skin. There was something deeper there. It was that the mere fact of her being a woman had so incensed this man that he had sought to destroy what *made* her a woman. He had attacked her where she was usually the most beautiful, confident and empowered, by deriding her body and the beautiful things that she did with it. *You are good for nothing but sucking my cock. You may be smarter than me, more attractive than me, and more accomplished than me, but I can still get a hard-on and demean you with my genitalia.* Life loses some of its shine when we are faced with the unprovoked meanness of strangers. The attack of a coward. A man making himself feel better about himself by making a woman feel worse about herself. Eventually my anger dissipated, or transformed into contempt, disgust. I took off my work clothes and slipped into my pyjamas. I turned the light off and wrapped myself around Angela's body, enfolding her protectively in my arms.

* * *

When David arrived for his weekly counselling session he was fifteen minutes late and looked uncharacteristically furtive. We chatted for a while, and I tried to steer the conversation to thoughts and feelings, but David's heart just wasn't in it. I didn't push him. There would be other sessions for that. So instead, we sat together quietly for the most part, glancing off the simple topics like sport and weather. David's mood changed suddenly when Evie swanned in and blew me a kiss. She acknowledged David with an 'Oh hello' and a little wave and then watched with me as David blushed, rose quickly from his chair, said good-bye, and walked out into the street. To fill the silence Evie observed, 'He's sweet.' I turned to look at her. I said nothing. 'What?' she demanded smugly. I watched her carefully and she squirmed under my gaze. She was a hopeless liar. A few quiet seconds and then Evie rolled her eyes and shook her head and blurted out, 'So he visited me at the brothel. What's the big deal?' I risk-assessed the information silently but knew intuitively that this was a bad thing for David. I was thinking 'Oh God no' but all I said was, 'Did you do it?' Evie shrugged like it was not important. 'It was only a hand job,' she muttered finally, in exasperation.

So that made it Evie 1 and Gregory nil then.

*   *   *

Weren't we good! We were so *wholesome*. Tuesday prayer group. It was the chit-chat in the minutes before we all took our seats and the session started. Twenty-five people had formed little clusters of conversation around my lounge room. Some held Bibles. Everyone was so clean that they gleamed. Their eyes, their smiles, their modest blouses buttoned to the neck. There was no cleavage. There were no swear words. No rude talk. No innuendo. No edge. Our room was a cocoon of safety and seemliness. We were all as harmless and as pure as raw oats. De-sexed like infants, we discussed gladioli bulbs, sponge cake, the new patio. The goodness treacled around the room like warm saliva. Some sing-song and happy-clapping, some Bible reading and prayer, then cakes and tea and more goodness. Yes, we were just so fucking *nice*. But you should have heard them on the subject of women who've had abortions.

*   *   *

One night at The Mission, I introduced Angela to Mister Theory, and for the next ten minutes I ceased to exist for her. It was like a switch had been flicked. No words were spoken to me, no laughter was shared with me. Instead, Angela had eyes, rolling eyelid-fluttering eyes, only for Mister Theory who stood before her impassively, receiving each touch and flirtatious giggle with a light meaningless half-smile. Angela used the vocabulary of a sexually charged language. A mix of body contact, eye contact and innuendo, an odd combination of sexual precociousness and submissiveness. It was painful for me to watch because although

I knew that this was some kind of game to Angela, one with rules and an outcome that were beyond me, it felt like she had *decided* to act this way, and therefore that she had decided to hurt me. Excluded, marginalised, disfavoured, I felt humiliated in front of my friend. My friend, however, who surprised me. Mister Theory at first confused and then infuriated Angela by being completely unresponsive. Later, when Angela left in a poorly disguised huff, I could tell that Mister Theory believed he had her all worked out. He was too fond of me to say what he was really thinking. I pressed him. Finally, he conceded, 'You've got your hands full there, mate.'

* * *

I felt like one of those praying mantises whose hips keep going long after the head has been gnawed off. I was having sex with Angela. We had had an argument that afternoon and Angela thought it was make-up sex. It was not. My cock was hard and my pelvis was thrusting against hers, but I felt nothing. If she could have seen my face, my forehead resting on the pillow under her own head, she would have seen dispassionate eyes. I fucked and fucked, maintaining a mechanical rhythm. She was wet and slippery, and writhed with her eyes closed in all the right places. And she came, or gave a good impression of it. The praying mantis kept fucking for a bit, then stopped and withdrew his penis. Angela opened her eyes. 'You're not coming?' she asked, confused. I shrugged, shaking my head. 'I don't feel like it,' I told her. She looked hurt. Revenge.

* * *

In the church hall before the morning service one Sunday I stood by the window gazing absently into the car park. I sensed movement beside me and turned to see Mary standing there. She seemed tired and drawn. Even after all this time I felt the need to hold her. She smiled. 'Well, I've missed you,' she told me candidly then averted her eyes momentarily. 'You can be a bit of a bastard but you're a good shoulder to cry on too.' She trailed off. The things that I wanted to say! *Come to me. Let me embrace you. Let me hold you until all pain ceases to exist.* But all I could do was nod and smile and chat for a couple of minutes until Gregory joined us, breaking the circle we could have formed. We separated and walked to our seats and as we parted I felt a pang of longing. Not for sex. That was behind us by then. We had passed an irrecoverable point. No, it was that Mary seemed so weary, and because I read need in her eyes. I was vain enough to think that I was at the heart of it. I didn't yet understand that I was barely even a shade of its colour.

* * *

I felt pangs of longing for Mary. I missed her. But I was also reminding myself that I was the luckiest man alive. My understanding girlfriend was gorgeous. She was sexy. Men desired her. Men envied me.

I was lying in bed on a Saturday morning at this time. The sun was clear and warm. Angela was in the bathroom showering. I could hear her singing to herself, snatches of some silly tune. She sounded like a young girl, singing songs from her teen years with soppy and sentimental lyrics. The water splashed onto the tiled floor as she bent and lathered and moved about the shower recess. It was the sound of post-coital bliss. A woman washing her sensuous body, erasing me lovingly.

I rolled out of bed and strolled into her lounge room. There was a TV in one corner on an old 1970s coffee table. No lounge in the lounge room, just bean bags and fat cushions. Lots of books by formidable authors – Plato, Dostoevsky, Foucault – sitting cheek by jowl with trashy magazines padded out with photographs of American movie stars and pop singers in various stages of binge and purge. The mind of woman is a mystery. I felt comfortable there after all these weeks of boyfriendedness so I flicked through her belongings without thinking. I was certainly not prying. I was just a little curious really. So I crouched in front of her bookshelves and looked her collection over, and absently opened the drawers built into one side of it. More pulp mags mixed with old notebooks, telephone books and newspapers. I spied a DVD and picked it up. It was a porn flick! This surprised me and maybe even aroused me a little. The movie was called *Holey Moley*. A 'portfolio' of 'holes' was exhibited on the back. There was a photograph on the front cover of a pretty young girl on the edge of a bed, legs and lips splayed, man to her right feeding his appendage into her mouth. I looked at the photograph and it dawned on me slowly. It was hard to tell at first because the girl was in profile and her face was showing the strain of simultaneously twisting to the side and fitting a very big nob in her mouth. But there was no mistaking it. It was Angela.

I didn't know what to do. I was aghast. I felt shock, jealousy, anger, sorrow. I looked on the back of the cover. Made three years ago, when Steve was still on the scene. I scrutinised the front cover again. That was definitely Steve providing the penis. I was still debating how to tackle the situation when I heard a noise behind me and turned to see Angela. She was wrapped in a towel, boobs and hips covered. She looked very matronly and conservative but when she saw the DVD in my hand she became something else. A small child. She shed years before my very eyes. She embodied the anguish that only a child can. She put a hand to her mouth. She did not speak. She did not run to me. She did not snatch it from my hand and throw the DVD against the wall. She did not cry. She did not show anger at me for prying. But her face was all anguish and loss and horror. Her wide eyes held mine and she pleaded with me softly, 'Please don't look at it!' I stood up to go to her. 'Oh pleeease,' she begged, 'put it away.' And so in spite of myself, in spite of my own fears and doubts and confusions, I held her to my body as she wept. Big gulping sobs. 'He made me do it,' Angela told me through hot, wet teardrops. Steve. And, she swore, it was the only one she ever made and she only slept with Steve. I told her over and over that it was alright, cooing softly and rocking her gently. I told her that I was not angry with her. I assured her that I would certainly not judge her for this thing. But I was missing the point. She was not ashamed. It was worse than that. It was only later that I put two and two together. She was feeling a pain that I couldn't understand yet. The pain created by the DVD derived not from shame but from *betrayal*. Steve and his cock in her mouth, the camera rolling, forcing her to do it when she had asked him, begged him, not to. I can barely imagine the anguish of her breaking heart.

Angela sobbed herself to a sniffy silence after a few minutes. I held her throughout. Her towel had fallen from her body and was a manky pile on the floor. It was the loveliest of all nudity, comfortable and companionable. She looked up at me with pinkish eyes and asked, 'Do you still love me?' I had never told her that I loved her. Her question was a brave one, but she had read me well. 'Yes,' I replied and kissed her tenderly.

* * *

Ah, the magic of photography. Having seen my girlfriend give her ex-boyfriend a blow job I felt that we had reached a point of familiarity where it was only right that I should spend more time with her in public. Unfortunately, however, Angela had developed a particular hankering. She suggested that she come to church with me one Sunday to watch me give a sermon. As my blood turned to ice-water in my veins, she smiled at me encouragingly, then frowned and said, 'Aw, c'mon. It'll be fun. What are you worried about?' Angela was sitting at the breakfast table eating Weet-Bix. She was fully clothed, if anything she was demurely dressed, and yet even just doing *that*, she somehow managed to look sexual. I shuddered to think what they would make of it at the church if she walked in on my arm. I stuttered excuses. Angela listened in silence. 'Forget it,' she said curtly, but Angela hadn't forgotten. Two days later she walked through my front door half an hour before Tuesday prayer group was due to start. Normally she worked on Tuesday evenings but in any case we had previously agreed that Tuesday nights were a no-no. Before I could say anything, Angela had strolled past me, hips swaying provocatively, and walked into the bedroom. She called over her shoulder, 'I thought I'd lie in here for a couple of hours and read a book.' The door closed behind her and locked. Ten minutes later, Donna was at the front door.

Prayer group passed like a kidney stone. The singing, the Bible reading, the prayers, the cakes, the whole bloody lot, carried out in a cold sweat of anxiety. I expected the door to burst open at any moment to reveal a scantily clad Angela beckoning with bent index finger. *Come and get it, big boy.* Amen. Cakes finished, I practically pushed the lingerers out the front door, passing them their coats, smiling weakly, corralling them on the front step. Finally, I was alone in the lounge room. There was silence. I heard my bedroom door open a crack and Angela's little voice say, 'Can I come out now?' When I meekly said yes, she emerged from the bedroom slowly, looking thoughtful. 'That was weird,' she said quietly, then after a moment of distractedness she pecked me on the cheek and sat on the edge of the lounge. Angela had finally seen that there were two Simons, and that she had some competition. She sat there with her knees drawn up looking scared, maybe even jealous. And so she should have been. She was beginning to see that she was competing for my affections with a God that neither of us even believed in.

* * *

A few days later, Angela made a point of telling me that the man from the travel agency across the road had asked her out to the movies. It was important to her that I knew. She watched my face carefully for the reaction. She registered my poorly concealed irritation with a microscopic upwards twitch at the corner of her mouth.

* * *

At the same time, Gregory was working on David's sense of guilt. He didn't know that David had recently been very expertly manually pleasured by a prostitute but he knew that every young man has thought about being very expertly manually pleasured by *somebody.* So Gregory said, 'I worry, David. I worry.' Shaking his head, he gestured with his hand to the street outside and said, 'You're a good boy, David, a good good boy, but I worry for you because this is no place for a *good* boy. These women, these prostitutes …' His voice trailed off as he searched theatrically for words. 'They ply a *foul* trade. They will muddle the mind of a boy like you, David. They will try to corrupt you, lad. I worry that one of these girls will one day try to take advantage of your good nature.'

As Gregory spoke, I watched David's shoulders slump under the weight of his shame, but I only saw it for a short time, because gradually his body language began to change. After a few seconds David's shoulders straightened and a new emotion settled. He began to look angry and reproachful, no longer ashamed, but he was not angry with Gregory, he wasn't reproaching himself. Quite the opposite. In fact, Gregory had saved him. He had given David the salve for his guilt. Although it was David who had looked up the brothel's address in the phone book, and although it had been David who had made the appointment, who had entered the boudoir, and who had come in Evie's hand, Gregory had told him that it was all okay. He had told David that it wasn't, in fact, David's fault. It was the whore's fault. It wasn't the man's fault. It was poor Evie's.

Summer

So David was one of the reasons that I knew what I was doing to Angela was wrong. I knew where I was letting her down. I knew it but couldn't stop it. I didn't actually *want* to stop it. I was punishing Angela. I was making her pay for being sexy and pretty, and I was doing that because it hurt every time that she flirted with another man. Every time that she made eyes at some other fellow at a party I felt the stab in my side. It was all harmless fun to her, a harmless little power trip. That's clear to me now. She was getting her own back. A neat trick of revenge for every man that had ever slipped her DVD into their computer drive and masturbated over her abused image. Her flirting was her own little joke at their expense. She was holding her body before them, the most delicious and attractive of all baits, and she was teasing them with it. What was once abused had become a potent weapon. She got them hard and then at the end of the evening, when they were drunk, when the hormones were pulsing, she pulled herself together with a certain haughtiness and walked away from them, hips swaying seductively. And she left with *me*, and a cheeky glance over her shoulder. She was saying, 'You may want it but you can't have it. It is my choice, and I choose this man.' I should have been feeling pretty good about that.

But didn't that just make me part of the power play? Didn't it make me another weapon? Is that what the sex was all about? No. Her message was lost on me. I didn't want her body to be a weapon. I didn't want it to tease and tickle and then deprive. I wanted her sitting with me and being kind. I wanted her warm hand resting on mine. I wanted her to peck me on the cheek from time to time and I wanted the world to see her do it. If there was any flirting to be done it could be done with me! Because sitting at some party all on my own for hours while Angela teased and tickled her way to empowerment in a gaggle of stupid men, I was being judged. The men were looking at me as if to say, 'How can you let her do that to you?' and I had no answer for them. They wouldn't have understood the need she had to take back her body at the expense of bad men's egos. They just saw a girlfriend playing up on her boyfriend and it was killing me. I wanted her to stop. I wanted her to grow up. I wanted it to stop hurting. And so I started to punish her. I became surly. I withheld cuddles. I deliberately didn't notice when she bought a new dress. I stopped telling her that she was beautiful. Even when I wanted to cuddle and compliment her I would let her feel the chill arctic breeze of my anger. But I wouldn't talk to her about it either. It's not that I was a man and therefore inarticulate. I had the words for my pain. It's that to express them gave her another little victory over men. This time, me. And I didn't deserve to be vanquished. You see, she was becoming cruel too. She was becoming the abuser. And frankly, she shouldn't have needed me to tell her when I was feeling hurt. Because I loved her. I had *told* her that I loved her. And in love there should be no power. There should be no games. There should be no torment. Love is the opposite of the exercise of power. It is about relinquishing it.

And yet there was Angela at barbecue after barbecue, party after party. It hurts even now to recall it. She sat in lap after lap, gazed up into eyes, flirted and giggled. All the laps enjoyed it, I remember that much. Granted, she left with me each time. We went home together and made love as often as not. Sure, in leaving, there was power over that man's lap. But in making me watch it, there was cruelty. And all cruelty is power.

So that's how it went, building up to a big head of steam, reaching an inevitable kettle-whistle of hurt and resentment. After one of these parties we went home together where I scowled about the kitchen, pretending to make a cup of tea, finding excuses not to go to Angela who was in the bedroom. I was angry and she knew why. I was hurt. She was ruining everything for both of us. Finally, Angela appeared in the doorway in her undies, no bra. She rested one hand on the door jamb and watched me for a while with an indulgent eye. She smiled and walked across the room to me, wrapping her arms around my waist. She was ready to make up. Her gestures illustrated it with trust, inviting me to be a part of her again. 'Come on,' she said. 'Let's go to bed.' But I was not ready to give up my anger yet. I aimed for where I knew it hurt. 'Ready to stop acting like a little tart then?' I snapped at her. I felt Angela's arms unloop from my waist. She stepped back, aghast. I had seen that look before. When I had last seen it I'd had a DVD in my hand. I stepped towards her to apologise but she had already started walking for the bedroom, where she would dress before walking silently out the door.

* * *

It was not over but there began a definite cooling off. Over the following three weeks there had been fewer phone calls, fewer spontaneous kisses on the mouth, no love-making. Angela was hurt and I couldn't blame her. Of course, I was hurt as well but I was the one that cracked first. More than anything on earth I wanted to make it right again. So I spent the day at The Mission rehearsing what I would say. It all involved abasing myself. I would apologise. I would seek forgiveness. I would hold her and comfort her because I missed her terribly. I would tell her that, pour out my heart. It never entered my mind that there could be anything wrong with this scenario. It never occurred to me that she may have made other plans.

I dropped by at Zanadu. Angela blushed when I entered the shag palace but we were both polite and strangely a little distant. We made small talk for a while. I watched her face intently. She liked me a lot, a hell of a lot, I just knew it. I could tell by her look and her manner. Gradually we started to reconnect during the conversation. A little joke. A little smile. And finally, one more lame joke, and Angela laughed, stepped out from behind the counter and gave me a big warm hug. I could feel her cheek against my chest. My heart was thumping. What relief. What wonder that her embrace could make me so damn happy. And what joy that I could now love her again. I would have done just about anything for her at that time. Anything. I asked her whether she'd like to stay the night at my place. 'Yes,' she said and my spirits soared. She would be round after work in a couple of hours, she told me. I kissed her and she let me. I would never hurt her again, not as long as I lived.

A couple of hours later there was a tap at my door and Angela came in sheepishly. We made love. Quiet and restrained. In my dim bedroom, illuminated by the light in the lounge room, we held each other and rocked together. It was the sex that two loving friends share. It meant something. We knew each other's bodies so intimately by then that there were few mysteries. Yet this made it the antithesis of boring. Knowing the responses of your partner and the touch that excites them, every act is measured to bring the other person pleasure. The act becomes a gift that is embellished and returned by the loving other. Afterwards I lay beside her and thanked my lucky stars. But I was setting myself up for a fall.

The next morning I woke to birds chirping in the morning sun from the trees outside the window. I left the bed and visited the toilet. The body always lets you down! When I returned, Angela was lying tangled in the sheets sleeping. She was on her side, one leg under the sheets and the other on them. She sensed my movements in her sleep and rolled over onto her back. She was immodest in her sleep. Her legs were open, creamy white. I could see the inside of her pale thigh, high up. This was my favourite part of her body. Soft and smooth beyond measure. I often touched her there with the pad of my index finger. With barely any pressure the flesh would give under the fingertip's nothing-weight. Can a person's body really be so perfect? I let my eye linger for a moment on that delicate and intimate place and noted the paling dark blemish of the love bite there. The love bite. It dawned on me in a cold wave. What fucking love bite? I hadn't been down there like that for the last three weeks!

So you see? Do you see how easy it is that a world can collapse?

I needed to handle it carefully. I needed to think it over. Take it slowly. So what did I do? I shook Angela awake and as she struggled to focus her sleepy eyes I pointed at her fanny accusingly and demanded, 'What the fuck is that?!'

*　*　*

She started out with confected outrage, which was a bad tactical move because it made me mean. For the whole conversation, if it can be called that, she was on the verge of tears, but it didn't stop me. I was in the right. We both knew it. And yet even at that moment, even with the image of some bastard putting his face between her legs and nibbling her delicious thighs, even with my heart shrieking in pain, I felt greater love for her than I had ever felt before. But it didn't stop me being mean. I inflicted pain with wounding words, and yet would have done anything to have taken it away from her as well. And through it all, my mind was reciting a silent prayer. Please please please, I thought over and over. Please let there be a sensible plausible explanation. Please. I wanted us to be laughing about this in five minutes time. But I also knew the truth. I knew that whatever happened from that moment on, things would be different between us. And so she denied it but when she finished extemporising an explanation we both knew how weak it sounded. There was no explanation for this. Pinching underpants! I mean, please!

And then she was silent for a long time. She too knew that she had hurt me. She too wanted to hold me. She too wanted this to disappear and for us to turn back the clock, recover the past, turn it into something else: forgetting. In the tense quiet bedroom our hearts beat out long pulsing dirges. We were both beyond words or gestures. I couldn't even bring myself to speak. She tried to touch my shoulder. Her hand rested there for a second but she felt something under her touch that made her withdraw her fingers. What she felt was white hot. It was not anger. What I felt at that moment was a long way from anger. It was in many ways its polar opposite. What I felt was a limitless sadness and hurt. I looked in her eye and saw the same thing there. I wanted to magnify it within her. Not because I am cruel but because I needed her to understand what she had done to me. To feel what I was feeling. I asked her to leave. She rolled from the bed without any clothes on, defenceless and exposed, and walked about the room collecting discarded clothing from the floor. I watched her. That would be the last time that I saw her body disrobed. She dressed, sobbing bravely on withheld tears. Then quietly she left the room. I heard the front door close after her. I lay back on the bed and waited for the pain to leave me. I would only have to wait about a lifetime for that.

*　*　*

Poor me. The victim of infidelity. The victim where I had always been the perpetrator. Some would find it hard to feel sorry for me, but I didn't. Selfishness, like love, is blind. So it was time to dig a hole. A deep dark dank miserable fucking hole. Fill it with something awful and wallow in it. I spent days in a horror world of despair. I couldn't get it out of my head. It swirled in there like some wasp-in-a-bottle dementia. An image. The image. Angela stripped naked and lying back for some man, opening her legs and letting him suck her inner thigh. What was she thinking? I *must* have crossed her mind. She *must* have thought of me, even for a moment, as the other man set to work on her delicate capillaries, and if that was the case, as it must surely have been, then she must have dismissed that thought. She must have *dismissed* me, at least long enough to let his slavering mouth bruise her. The pain was unbearable. A man can die of such pain. If only the image had stopped there. No, the love bite could only have been a prelude. His hands on her body. His fingers and cock. I felt the rage.

But mostly I felt the loss. In fact, I felt the worst of emotions. Worse than sadness and worse than embarrassment and worse than anger and worse than humiliation and worse than fear and worse than hate. Worse than all of these things because it is all of these things together, piled one on top of the other to create a new super-emotion that swamps the spirit. Jealousy. I was jealous.

I forced myself to go to work. The days passed me in a haze. I operated like a robot. I stood before the youth group and the prayer group and the Sunday sermons and words left my body and I didn't even know where they came from. My brain was operating according to its own rules. It was my old mate. It could tell that the rest of me was falling apart and proved to be the friend that helps by taking up the slack. Good brain, I owe you one. So I dealt with things by bottling it up and told myself I was toughing it out, but there was another reason for that. I still loved her of course. Or at least I thought I did. By bottling it up, I didn't have to tell people. Telling people that someone has cheated on you makes it an irrevocable thing, and irrevocability was the last thing that I wanted. Somewhere in my head I had formed a thought that we might even get back together!

Poor fool. Rumours began to filter through to me from some of the girls at the Cross. Angela had been seen with another man. They passed on the information kindly enough but they watched my face for the reaction. I steeled myself and asked for descriptions. He sounded familiar to me but I rejected the thought as unconscionable, a cruel under-estimation of Angela, but it was true. Another girl met them at the cinema and the new man had been introduced, the man who Angela opened her legs to, who pressed his rough bewhiskered mouth to her skin, and his name was Steve. Angela and Steve were back together! I received the news with resigned equanimity. I excused myself and took the bus home. The sorrow overwhelmed me as a kind of fatigue. Somewhere between the Cross and my bedroom I dessicated. All the moisture in my body left me. The juices that keep the cells going, the joints lubricated, the oxygen supplied, and my very soul alive, turned to ash and dust. I shrivelled into a tiny speck and blew about in the breeze.

*　*　*

And then happy-go-lucky Evie put an end to her happy-go-lucky life, although she didn't know it until a few months later.

Later, much later, she reconstructed the events for me. Poor Evie. Abused in childhood and washed ashore on the streets of Sydney she turned to prostitution so that she could be anywhere but at home. And while Angela and I punished each other over a love bite, things were turning sour across town for sassy Evie. Perhaps inevitably, certainly accidentally, and in spite of all precautions, Evie fell pregnant. As unsentimental as ever she procured an abortion, making no fuss about it, telling nobody. Nine days later, Gregory paid her a visit.

He tapped on her door and when she opened it, she let him in because he was irresistible in all the wrong ways. Someone in the Cross had told him what Evie had done and he was determined not to leave. She let him in simply because she hadn't the strength to fight him. Evie returned to her lounge where she had been watching television, curled up under a blanket. Her belly still aching with an unexpected sense of loss, Gregory coolly wore her down. He talked for three hours. A persistent rant delivered *sotto voce*. He told her that she had sinned. He told her that she was a sinner. He told her of the redemptive love of Jesus and the soul of her lost murdered baby. He told her that there is a special place in hell for abortionists. He told her that she could be saved. That she *needed* saving. Moron. He was too lost in his own prejudices to see that he was doing nothing more than introducing shame to Evie's sorrow.

Evie listened politely enough, excusing herself from time to time to gulp down another mug of whisky in the kitchen. She heard his words through a woolly fug. She tried to muffle his obsessive ranting with the booze but it served only to amplify all the worst aspects of it. Finally, even Gregory tired of himself. He told her he had to leave but would only do so if she promised to come to church with him the following Sunday. Evie made the promise blithely, never intending to fulfil it, and never in fact fulfilling it. The last she saw of Gregory was his big arse as he pulled the door closed after himself. Evie was a tiny lump under the blanket. An hour passed. Evie roused herself. She dressed. Miniskirt. Low-cut blouse. Fuck-me boots. Sheer cotton knickers. Then she headed into town for a shift at the knocking shop.

The usually confident, cocky Evie approached the brothel feeling cheap and mean. Her heels clacked on the footpath. It was a crisp whorey sound that she knew drew attention to her arse under that short skirt. She could smell her own body. She felt the opposite of sexy. She wished she'd worn a baggy old dress that day. She wanted no eyes on her boobs, no hands on her body. She wanted to disappear with a book, away from humans who would judge her. This was a new sensation for Evie, because she had never before feared judgement, least of all her own. But for the first time in her life she felt like she was somehow undeserving. The thought had not coalesced clearly in her mind. She didn't think to herself, 'I am worthless', but Gregory had had an impact. Sin. Whore. Abortion. Strong words that had diluted her. She had become tepid water. It hit her as a kind of emotional fatigue, a feeling in her heart and in the womb that it, everything, just wasn't worth the effort. She felt like her blood was thinner, that she was breathing thinner air. She just plain didn't care. Gregory had broken her where three years of prostitute users hadn't.

The first client went smoothly. Nothing out of the ordinary. She described the next one for me many months later, in a quiet voice, her face pale, hands trembling. The second client that evening would change her life forever, maybe even end it. Average height. Average weight. His chest and legs and genitals were covered in dark hairs. Evie began with a massage. This was standard. It came with the price. After a few minutes of that the punter rolled over and she saw his erection. A big rubbery cock poking out of a thatch of pubic hair. He asked her to suck him off but that was not part of the deal. It was a clean brothel. No oral without a rubber. He snorted his derision. 'Waste of fucking time,' he said. He ordered Evie brusquely to turn around. He wanted to do it from behind. She submitted to his probing fingers. She let him spread her cheeks. She was about to tell him that anal was not on either, that he should know the rules, when she felt him enter her vagina. Business as usual. How many times had she been in this position? Arse in the air. Anonymous cock inside her. Anonymous man bumping against her bum. In a sudden moment of self-awareness, Evie saw the whole thing through the eyes of others. She felt tears in her eyes. She felt disgust. Not for the man, who she merely registered as faintly ridiculous, but for herself.

She felt the man pull out and heard him pull the rubber off. She told him, 'No rubber, no sex.' But he told her that it was like fucking in a wetsuit, he couldn't feel a thing and that if she let him in without the condom he'd pay her an extra $500, cash in hand. 'Come on,' he said. And Evie barely thought it over. It wasn't the money. It was that she just didn't see herself as important enough. Who was she to make a fuss? What difference did it make anyway? What was the worst that could happen? Gregory had spent three hours that afternoon putting a value on her, and it was pretty fucking low.

Evie resumed the position. She felt the man insert two fingers inside her and move them in and out, working up her moisture. Her body responded in spite of itself. Then he penetrated her and began an aggressive rhythmic thrusting. He breathed heavily through his mouth throughout the sex act. He sniffed and cleared his throat like there was nobody else in the room. It was horrible. And then he came, withdrew, strolled to the wash basin, and washed his cock without a hint of embarrassment. He dressed, paid Evie her $500 and walked out to reception. He paid the standard fee there as well.

Alone on pink frilly sheets, Evie reached for the tissues. She stood beside the bed and half-squatting expelled the spoonful of semen from her body. More disgust, this time for the man as well as for herself. Then she dressed and headed into the tea room for a cuppa.

Later that night she slept with two more clients. They wore condoms. They were well behaved. And then Evie went home, cradling in her wounded womb the first dots of the virus that would eventually destroy her.

* * *

And while this was happening, another tragedy was unfolding on the other side of the city in Gregory's stuffy office. David described it for me later, his eyes shining, a dopey, evangelical grin plastered across his face. That night, Gregory had returned from the Cross feeling elated. Leaving Evie's lounge room, he buzzed with the Holy Spirit. He felt that he had struck a blow for God. Three hours of teaching a fallen woman how degraded she had become would make anybody feel good about themselves, wouldn't it? It was only going to get better for Gregory that night. David had made an important decision. As Gregory sat down at his desk, David tapped on his open door and was

God-bless-you-ed into the office. Seated opposite Gregory, clenched hands in his lap, David announced in hushed tones that he had decided to dedicate his life to Christ, that he wished to go to Bible College, where he would learn to love God and become a preacher. Gregory received the news in awed silence. His chest swelled inches. He rose from his chair, and with tears welling in his eyes, he moved around the desk to where David was sitting. David rose also and they embraced each other, a big hearty back-slapper. They stood together in each other's arms for half a minute, genitals uncomfortably aligned, surely. David was the prodigal son. Gregory was the father. Gregory muttered his thanks to God over and over again. They separated like they had achieved something, and Gregory raised his voice in a hallelujah. He wiped a manly tear from his eye with the back of his sleeve. He rested a hand on David's shoulder. He said, 'Praise Jesus', even as an anonymous punter, in a brothel in Kings Cross, came in Evie's damaged body.

Tragedy. A tragedy because David had been betrayed. A tragedy because Gregory had fooled David into believing that he was giving nothing away that wasn't cheap and foul and sinful and shameful, when in fact he was surrendering the passion that women can excite, and curiosity and exploration. He was passing up the joy and the excitement of discovery, the adrenal rush of undressing a woman the first time, meeting, seducing and being seduced.

Quite an achievement. In the space of an evening, Gregory had cheapened the bodies of two beautiful young people in their own eyes.

* * *

And as Gregory and David embraced each other so warmly in Gregory's office, outside a nightclub in the Cross a dark-coloured car sleazed down Darlinghurst Road. There were three men in it, two in the front and one in the back. Like all cowards they needed company. They were all big men with short cropped hair and tight t-shirts. The car slowed as it passed Cherry Pop, just as

Mister Theory was leaving the building. A single gunshot and Mister Theory fell to the ground with blood seeping through the fabric of his black shirt. The car accelerated, gears shishing between changes, and disappeared around a corner. Mister Theory heard the faint cheers of the three men. Their celebration. He was left crumpled on the footpath, his legs twisted beneath him, bewildered by the sudden change in his condition. He made to rise but his legs would have none of it. He closed his eyes and wondered if this was how he would die. He tried again to get up but couldn't. Two working girls ran to him, cradled his face in their laps, tears coursing down their cheeks, crying out in their horror and dismay.

I got the call an hour later from one of the girls from Cherry Pop. She could hardly speak she was crying so much but she eventually told me that Mister Theory had been rushed to the hospital where he had asked for me and only me. I was in Emergency twenty minutes later and was taken immediately to Mister Theory. He was lying on the bed braced in traction, lots of tubes and beeping machines hanging off him, his eyes closed. No-one deserved this. I moved to his side and held his hand. Mister Theory opened his eyes but he was only half there. They had drugged him up. He turned his head slightly when he felt my touch and gave me a faint smile. It was a smile that said, 'They got me'. He suspected but didn't yet know that he would never walk again.

* * *

And then Pru died. I got the call from Patti late in the day and rushed around to her place, my mind numbed and spinning. When she opened the door I half-expected her to fall into my arms a sobbing mess, but she didn't. Instead, she hugged me firmly and briefly, and led me into the lounge room, ushering me into my usual fat armchair. We sat opposite each other quietly for a while with the ghost of Pru in the room for company. Mechanically, resignedly, Patti told me what happened. Pru had cancer all along, vicious ugly little brain tumours, but she had wanted to keep that to herself. Two days earlier she had collapsed, complaining that she had no feeling down her left side. They called an ambulance but Pru was drifting into the coma even as they wheeled her into the vehicle. Two days in a floating semi-conscious state. And death.

I listened without a word as Patti related the story. Her voice trembled very slightly and her face registered a subtle and endearing sadness, but she held it together proudly. I felt the sorrow swelling in my own throat. There seemed to be just so much unfairness in the world. Patti saw me swallowing and walked across the room to put her arm around my shoulder. 'I'll miss her, Simon,' she said. 'I loved her dearly.' I sucked it in. If Patti could tough it out then so could I. 'But why didn't she tell us?' I half-whispered. Patti shrugged. She reached into her sleeve and extracted a tissue that she used to wipe her eyes. Finally she told me, 'Because she didn't want them to pray for her.'

Patti went to the drinks cabinet and poured us both a brandy. We sipped it in silence for a while, then Patti spoke, as though thinking aloud, 'You know, towards the end we talked about euthanasia. Pru was in a lot of pain but more than anything she feared that she'd lose control of her body. She was a very proud woman, Simon. She always lived with a great deal of dignity. She wanted to die with it also.' I said nothing. Patti took a deep breath and continued after another sip of brandy. 'I just couldn't do it, Simon. I just couldn't say good-bye that way. It was selfish but I loved her. Love, Simon. It's both the most selfless and selfish thing on earth.' Another sip of the brandy. 'In the end we didn't need to do it. The tumours took care of that. Thank God. Thank God.'

We lapsed into another silence. I could hear the clock on the wall ticking us away. Then a buzz and a cuckoo cooed the hour. Finally I said, 'I wish that I could have been there for her,' but Patti tutted me into silence. 'It would have been nice, Simon. She loved you. But ultimately we must all die alone.'

*   *   *

Misery and self-misery.

I was never one to console myself with booze, but I was always one to console myself with sex. Having lost all my safe harbours, my ports in the storms, I was at a loss. No Mary. No Faith. No Angela. I turned instead to King Street, Newtown, where I went like a predator to a waterhole. I knew I'd get laid. Getting laid is easy. All you have to do is not care. You just have to not give a shit any more. Not care if you hurt anyone. Not care about the cuddles afterwards. Not care about whether *she* doesn't care. It's all about using and not giving a lazy toss whether she is using you as well. It's about taking. Just think like a sociopath. Feel no regrets and no shame. And the women? They aren't hard to find. There is a lot of loneliness out there, patrolling bars, ranging across the dance floors, knocking back vodkas. They are there in their droves if you pick your mark. Drunk. Teetering on the edge of sentimentality. Vulnerable and hungry at the same time. Like you. Like me.

On King Street I found Grace. I met Grace in the Town Hall Hotel. Grace was womanly. A big female bum. Real hips and a waist. She wore a tight t-shirt. Her breasts were large. And she wasn't all that drunk. In fact, she seemed to be downright sober. If I were honest, I'd say she was a damn sight more sober than me. Good thing I didn't care. Good thing. We chatted. We laughed just enough to kid ourselves that we were connecting. Some body contact. Then she invited me back to her place. I went with her without even a scintilla of anticipation.

Grace had a hippy thing happening in the bedroom. Lots of tie-dyed fabrics and Pakistani carpets smelling of incense. Our move from her front door to her bedroom might have involved some unseemly haste, but what the hell. I came. She might have. Afterwards, I recall her half-lying and half-sitting and half awake, eyes closed, naked, propped up against the bedhead with a couple of pillows under her. Her big boobs had settled languorously on her ribs. I was sitting beside her with a nice view of them. I observed her nipples. They always come as a surprise to me. Endless variety, not just between women, sometimes between breasts on the same woman. But Grace, true to form when you consider her body as a whole, had the most womanly of nipples. They rested comfortably on her big breasts, breasts so heavy that the nipples themselves were not round but oval, stretched a little by the weight of them. They were dark, solid things. Brown, not pink. When they hardened they contracted from the edges of the areola, crinkling into firm urgent things that were resistant in the mouth. Harder than your tongue. Harder than your lips. Something you'd quite like to nibble on.

I reached out absently to touch them. They were sleepy. Soft. I tickled one with my fingertip and saw it stiffen (funny that the other stayed soft). And as I touched her I was thinking that it had been an *awful* week. I felt so sad. And my night with Grace was just me digging myself another horrible hole. I knew what I had done and registered it with shame. I had tried to battle my despair with the body of another person, uncaring and cruel. I had only made myself sadder and was probably making Grace sadder. I say 'sadder' because I could tell that she was also sad, although I don't know what was causing her brand of it. I hated myself for using. Using. Not drugs. Worse. Humans.

Grace started after a second or two of my touching. I had almost forgotten she was there. She looked at me with a mix of pity, anger and curiosity. 'What are you doing?' she demanded. I pulled my finger away in surprise. 'Nothing,' I said. I heard my voice from a distance. I sounded like a five year old with his hand caught in the biscuit jar. Grace relaxed a little. She looked down at her own boobs, then cupped them in her hands. Left in left. Right in right. She pressed them together and considered them nostalgically. 'They were nicer when I was young,' she told me softly. 'They're lovely now,' I said. And I meant it. But she shook her head dismissively and let them droop back down to their natural position. Droop. The word is appropriate but they were still beautiful. Her mood changed again. A sudden shift. An angry shift. I was a cock and balls again. 'I suppose you want to come on them or something,' she accused me, a weary angry tone in her voice. 'No', I told her without emotion. 'I just think they're lovely.' She considered for a moment, and then accepted the compliment for what it was. She lay back again as I leant towards her, letting her head rest against the bedhead. Leaning. Towards her. Towards them. She took her left breast in her right hand and fed the nipple into my mouth, as a mother would for a mewling, sucking infant.

* * *

The next few weeks passed in a muddy slush. I seemed unable to do anything at the old pace. Everything took an unfathomable amount of effort. I learnt that Angela had resigned from Zanadu and had moved. I heard nothing from her and was faintly disappointed. I was having trouble letting go and was objective enough to know how pathetic I was being. The knowledge did nothing to cheer me. Gregory on the other hand was bursting with energy as David became a more active member of the church. There were even rumours that Caroline with the bucked teeth was showing an interest. I hoped it was true and that her manual dexterity would not prove a disappointment for David who had experienced Evie's best work. I was hoping that Caroline might even screw him (and herself) out of this shit, but it was unlikely. They say there is none so righteous as the converted whore, but I reckon the timid and the weak come damn close to it. Gregory was after me to deliver more sermons but I called in sick two Sundays in a row. No-one seemed to see the irony in it. It wasn't so long ago that it was me who was healing the sick.

I saw nothing of Evie for a couple of weeks. Then I learnt that she had moved out of her place. I made enquiries and got no answers. I was told at first that she had moved to Melbourne. Another person told me she was home in Bathurst. A couple more weeks and she finally got in touch. She told me in a short and direct email that she was in fact home in Bathurst and wouldn't be back any time soon because she was HIV positive. The floor dropped out from under me again. I sent her a reply suggesting that I could come and visit but I got no reply. I seemed to have no-one to talk to. I told Gregory about Evie the following Sunday. He absorbed the news in silence, brows creased like the philosopher, but he automatically assumed that I had come to him for advice, an explanation, when all I needed was to share my concerns with another man who knew her. He began by observing that the Lord moves in mysterious ways, shaking his head in pseudo-consternation, but more than anything else, he seemed almost happy. The news was a vindication. I could see him thinking, 'See! I was right.' That afternoon he introduced Evie's illness to the congregation and invited their prayers, but Evie was just a subject, the moral at the heart of a trite parable. As Gregory talked I thanked his God that Evie was not there to see their pity. She would have been enraged. As I was.

I kept telling myself that I could get things all back to normal, but of course, it could never be the same again. I tried to contact Faith but had no luck. An acquaintance at the church told me that they had heard that she had been unwell and was holidaying in Switzerland. I still saw Mary often. She passed me at church and gave me soft sympathetic looks. We rarely spoke. Finally, I called her but she was kindly dismissive. I asked if we could meet but Mary sounded every bit the mother when she replied firmly but without rancour, 'No, Simon.' It didn't even occur to me that maybe Faith and Mary had their own troubles then, and I was no part of them, or of the solution.

And so with no friends in my own church I found myself almost every evening dropping in on Mister Theory at the rehab centre. I would sit to the side in a squeaky gym as he was taught how to use his chair or lay on his back bench-pressing weights to get strength back into his withered upper body. He had lost his old certainty. His skin bore a sickly pallor. But he was a friend. And then Mister Theory left too. His brother flew in from Perth. His wheelchair was packed into a station wagon, and he was carried like a child to the passenger seat. We shook hands through the window and I was left standing on a footpath, alone.

*   *   *

Four more weeks of that. Then one Tuesday prayer group and I couldn't help but notice a new face in the crowd. She didn't bake. I didn't even have to ask. It was obvious from her high heels and her demeanour. She sat erect in her seat looking amused but attentive, her long elegant spine curving to the tail bone, her hair gathered into a bun on her head, skewered with a hair pin. She wore understated stylish jewellery, a silk scarf around her throat. She was very pretty. I could feel her eyes on me when I spoke. When I looked at her she was looking at me and I caught her out. She didn't seem too concerned and we smiled to each other politely. We had passed an important irrecoverable milestone. At cake time she was introduced to me as Madeleine, Donna's sister, visiting from Brisbane where she owned a recruitment agency, whatever the fuck that is. She was a pleasant distraction. We passed a harmless half-hearted half minute of flirting before she left, plain Donna standing at her sister's shoulder all the while, a smile on her face like a grimace, brooding with Cain-like resentment.

* * *

A few more weeks of wading through something like life, then just when I thought it couldn't get any worse, it did. One early Sunday morning Gregory invited me to the Church Retreat. Oh. Fuck. Me. How could he not have noticed the anguish in my expression when I said yes? How could a man of the cloth cause so much pain? I dreaded the Church Retreat. It was Gregory's way of conveying a sense of what eternity feels like. Every year carefully selected members of his congregation would be bundled into mini-buses like POWs then shunted to remote locations in the country to 'bond'. The whole idea was based on the corporate experience, the brainchild of some American who doubtless figured it would get him laid. If it wasn't so close to Satanism there would have been walking across hot coals at the Church Retreat. It had been suggested that we give paintball a go but a party-pooper was worried about the militant overtones so instead it was decided that we'd sit in a room and talk about the Bible and why sexy people go to hell. The Church Retreat that year was to be held at a camping ground in the country. With shared accommodation. I received the news with a sense of impending doom. Even the other preachers, the ones that really practised charity and forgiveness, seemed a little perturbed. Because it was well known that blokey big-bummed Gregory liked to walk around communal all-male living spaces in his undies.

There were twenty of us at the Church Retreat that year. The agenda was distributed on the bus as we left Sydney and when there was no chance of escape. I ran my eye over it. Upon arrival we would be greeted by someone with a big smile and shown to our accommodation. We would then gather in the community hall for a prayer session and discuss 'Outreach' and 'Giving it up to God' into the evening. The following day involved a mystery activity. (They didn't know it but the mystery would be how I'd make it through the day without taking my own fucking life.) The afternoon would be dedicated to 'Scripture', 'Charity Work' and 'Evangelising'.

All the way there I stared morosely out the window. We ground through Sydney traffic for over an hour and then raced down the highway for another two. I saw nothing. I felt nothing. By the time we pulled up at the camping ground I had reached a decision. I'd see it through for the next two days, then on my return to Sydney I would find another job, my own home, and resign my commission with the Ministry of Christ. Getting off the bus I felt a sense of incredible relief. My relief evaporated when we were told that we would be sleeping in tents, one person per tent. Uncomfortable, but at least we would be spared Gregory's big girl's bum in its underpants. I dumped my bag inside one of the tents and we all strolled back to the community hall for the praying and talking.

Inside the hall, twenty chairs had been arranged in a circle. Finding myself a seat I took a look at the crowd. There were the preachers, some Elders, and representatives of the 'Women's Circle', 'Young Teens for Christ', and the 'Youth Group'. Gregory led us in prayer and then introduced us to the one stranger in the hall, a toothy man described as 'the facilitator', named Brett. I found myself tuning in and out of a conversation about God. The others would speak about him like he was somebody they used to have over for dinner. They knew what his thoughts were on an astonishing range of subjects. Abortion, euthanasia, Islam, everything. In despair I looked around the circle of the deluded and settled on the girl from youth group. Maybe nineteen years old. The complexion of a virgin. Selected for the Church Retreat for her charity work. In fact, if her posture were any indication, if she got any more bored she would have slipped into a coma. But I was surprised when she held my gaze and even gave me a little smile. Suddenly we were sharing a secret. Suddenly things were looking up.

And so. *This* is how it all went pear-shaped: I returned the little smile and burrowed back down into my own thoughts. My mind switched off. The chatter about God happened somewhere in the distance, like heavy furniture bumping around upstairs. It was a muffled drone, soft-edged. I took deep breaths and sighed. I'd had enough. I'd just plain had enough. Enough of the trite homilies. Enough of the sanctimonious head shaking. Enough of the smug finger wagging. I just didn't need it any more. And enough of the opposite pole. Enough vaginas. Enough tits. No more arses. I was sick of them all. Fed up. Prayer and sex. God and cunt. Boring. I was on the cusp of making a new and life-changing resolution when I glanced across the group again at the girl with the smile. She instantly put paid to that idea about new resolutions. She had slumped down into her seat like she'd been anaesthetised, her knees parting slightly with every inch further that she slumped. It's that easy. I was still off God but vaginas were back on the menu.

I marvelled. Surely she knew that her legs were open. I know when *my* legs are open and I don't wear a skirt. Or have a vagina. So why was it that this girl, a paragon of virtue from the Ministry of Christ youth group, was slumping in her seat across the circle of Christians from me with her knees splayed provocatively? I looked around the circle and the thought crossed my mind, for the briefest second, that perhaps I was the one with the problem. After all, nobody else in the room seemed to have noticed. Gregory sat near me banging away about why the Catholics had it all wrong. Even Donna looked bored. Legs Akimbo crossed her arms over her chest and looked down her nose at herself.

I tried to work out how old she was. Nineteen? Maybe. I looked again. I tried to tell myself that it was possible that she was older than nineteen and just looked young for her age. No, if that were the case would she be in youth group? She was young alright. A youth. Christ! Could I if she would? I mentally shrugged my shoulders. Who am I kidding, I asked myself. But then what did it matter anyway? I was off women, relationships, sexual salves to my problems. Right? But then, I told myself, I may as well fantasise while I'm listening. I was capable of it. I had done it a million times. The pious facial expression, the head tilted slightly to the side as if I were cocking an ear the better to hear, while in my mind I'm taking down my trousers and easing out that wobbly erection. From time to time I glanced across at Legs Akimbo and wondered if, maybe, it was just youthful innocence after all. Maybe. As I was thinking these thoughts through Gregory asked her a question because he wanted the perspective of 'someone a little younger than the rest of us'. Legs Akimbo brought her thighs together with an audible slap and sat up straight in her chair. I can't deny that I was a little disappointed.

We all turned to Legs Akimbo. She fumbled out an answer about something. I listened for a while, but then I tuned out again. Bored. Bored now her legs were closed again. I was looking out the window when I became aware that Gregory was wrapping things up. I ran my eye around the circle one last time. Gregory with his Bible open. Donna amen-ing. Legs Akimbo's knees had fallen apart again with the relief but although, if I'd had a mind to, I could have snatched a sneaky peek at her crotch lurking there crocodilian in the shadow of her skirt, I turned my thoughts instead back to Mary and Faith and everything that I had lost. To my own stupidity. My failings. The sense of overwhelming loss that I felt. Then, after a time, of course, I got a grip and took that sneaky peek.

Dinner was a fry-up around a campfire at dusk. It was all very wholesome, to be sure, but I made my excuses when the guitar made an appearance and strolled down to the creek behind the camp site. I needed time to myself. I had outgrown these people and my deceptions. At the creek I stopped under a grand

River Red Gum, crossing my arms against the cool evening. I literally shook my head to clear my thoughts as I breathed in the dry eucalyptus air. I remained there for ten minutes watching the day fade away. I heard movement behind me and turned to see a woman approaching confidently through the scrub.

It was Legs Akimbo. She walked up and stopped very close to me. I could see small speckles of light in her eyes. She was much shorter than me, which is really all that it took. She didn't have to do anything more than that. She just had to look tiny and little and cuddly and like something you'd want to defend manfully. She just had to do that thing. She just had to tilt her head back and look into my eyes. She did it. Big dark eyes. That, I must confess, had the desired effect. More to the point she was clearly absolutely aware of it. She *knew* that her eyes were sparkling. She *knew* that the head tilted back thing works wonders. She was playing on it. And it was no coincidence that tilting her head back also thrust her boobs forward provocatively. They didn't *quite* touch my arm but I could feel their warm presence. Whoops. She tripped a bit, accidentally, on purpose. I felt them that time. Oh God! Think of The Mission! Think of the good work that you could still do. Don't throw it all away for more of the same. But it was no use. I could hear the toilet flushing.

'What are you up to?' she asked, like I was keeping a secret. I told her that I was just taking in the night air and she seemed to find that very amusing. 'What's so funny?' I asked her and she told me that I was cute because I was so old-fashioned. That did wonders for my ego. I had been fifteen years older than her thirty seconds before. Suddenly I was her grandfather. She put her hands behind her back and stood on tip toes. The tits again. She wanted to watch it! Dangerous territory, but Legs Akimbo told me innocently that she loved the bush and she loved the native animals you get in the bush. She listed them for me: kangaroos, koalas, possums. She ran out of marsupials at possums. She screwed her face up, thinking, then shrugged. I guess she wasn't really all that worried about how many animals there were out there. There was a pause. I wanted to ask her how she felt about ticks because if I'd had my way right then she'd have been lying down in the scrub with me naked, risking a serious infestation. But of course she knew that too. I know she knew that because after a few more minutes of meaningless chit-chat she turned to me, unbuttoned her shirt, and opened it for me. She shucked it off her shoulders, reached around behind her back, unclasped her bra and let her boobs fall out. The bra dropped to the ground with the shirt. So, not too fussed about ticks then.

They were happy, playful breasts. Small and perky. She put her hands around my neck and kissed my mouth. Her nipples pressed against my chest, her mouth was delicious and warm and moist. She wasted no time. Maybe I *was* old-fashioned. I was certainly taken aback when she unbuckled my belt in one smooth practised motion, unbuttoned my shirt and unzipped my trousers. In a second no-nonsense move she had my jeans down around my ankles. My dick was in her mouth in no time, but I didn't put it there. That was all her doing, God bless her. But oh my God! Where did she learn how to do that stuff? Youth group? Two hours earlier she had been praising the Lord and singing hallelujahs, now her head was bobbing up and down on my willy energetically with little squelching noises for accompaniment. Bob-bob-bob. I had to admire her dedication. She never missed a beat. Was it all that singing practice? She had what Mister Theory would have described as perfect hand–mouth co-ordination and it did it for me. My knees gave out and I sagged to the ground with her following me with her head. Suddenly she disengaged from the end of my knob and looked up as if she'd just had a great idea. 'Hey, do you wanna come in my mouth?' she said wide-eyed.

'Yes please' seemed a little formal in the circumstances so I groaned my assent, my hands doing their own wandering now. She undid her trousers, kicked them off, put my right hand between her legs and shifted her pelvis obligingly. She was now completely naked with my penis in her mouth. Somebody could have walked in on us at any moment and I frankly couldn't have given a shit. I called to mind the day's prayer sessions and her provocative open crotch displays and the mere thought of it had the desired effect. I started to come. It raced up at me and I didn't fight it. I went with it. Fuck The Mission. Fuck the church. Fuck

Gregory and his lectures and fuck the whole fucking lot of them. I had seen too many people falling backwards lately and where were the people who were supposed to catch them? The ones with charity in their hearts, and with money in their middle-class pockets? And all through this, all through *it*, the girl's head bobbed up and down on me. She hung in there with feisty little sucky noises and as the whole sordid thing came to its sorry sticky end she looked up at me and looked very *very* pleased with herself. 'Can you do *me* now?' she asked matter-of-factly.

Later we lay together under the big River Red Gum as the hormones subsided. Now that the thrill had gone, the anxiety crept up the creek bed like a cold mist, settling in my marrow, and I found myself thinking, 'Now I am worried. I am *very* fucking worried.' Firstly, there were the ticks. And then there was the possibility that this woman would blackmail me then dob me in anyway. I would never work in The Mission again, or as a counsellor. Legs Akimbo seemed to sense my concern. She sat up and turned to look me in the face. 'Calm down,' she said as if I was a child, but also a little angrily. 'I'm not going to tell anyone.' She shook her head as if I was the dimmest person on earth. She put her head against my chest and said, 'I *wanted* to do it, dummy.' I wanted to say many things but thought better of it. Suddenly a thought occurred to me. I asked her her name. She allowed herself to get a little irritated. 'Sylvia,' she told me in an angry low tone. 'I know your first name, Sylvia,' I lied. 'I can't remember your last one.' It was Cunningham. I glanced down at Sylvia. She really did look stunning, naked in the moonlight. I made a light-hearted joke of what we had done. 'Are we going to hell?' I asked her. 'No,' Sylvia said with unaffected certainty. I was suddenly interested. 'Why's that then?' Sylvia was brushing a patch of dirt off her tummy. 'Because there isn't one,' she replied casually, without even looking up.

* * *

The next morning my mind was liquid with the questions. It's good isn't it? Isn't it? But of course it wasn't. I had just flushed years of hard work down the drain. I had betrayed, for a head job, all of those people at the Cross who needed me. The poor, the hungry, the addicted, the lost. So many negative emotions to choose from, that I hardly knew where to start. Guilt. Shame. Horror. I settled on the most primordial: abject terror. For a time I forgot my earlier certainties. Suddenly, l didn't want to be caught. I wanted to wind the clock back, return to The Mission and do good work for the needy, fake the prayer, eat scones at Tuesday prayer group.

I lay in my tent at dawn listening to the early risers stoking the fire for a brew-up. Oh Jesus. Fucking. Christ. I slipped out of my sleeping bag and dressed reluctantly, crouched over in the tent, psyching myself for the moment I would leave my safe little cocoon. A couple of deep breaths. Finally I unzipped the tent flap and stepped into the early morning. I didn't know where to look. I had nowhere to put my hands. A couple of coffee drinkers looked up and said 'hi' cheerily but a voice in my head was saying, 'They know. They must know.'

I could hear waking up noises emanating from the other tents. Coughing and groaning, sleeping bags unzipping. Faces emerged from tents first, bloodshot eyes and creased faces. The women looked the worst for some reason. I was offered a plate of eggs and sausages that were little more than congealed fat held together by sausage skin. I forked it into my dry mouth mechanically and glanced surreptitiously towards Sylvia's tent. I had just enough time to feel some guilt. I hoped I hadn't done any psychological damage to the poor kid. The tent zipper unzipped (a sound which brought back certain memories) and she stepped out of the dark interior looking puffy-eyed. I didn't want to be too obvious. I paid close attention to my grease. I was as cool as a cucumber but my heart was racing like a bastard. I knew that I would shrivel up and die if she walked over to me now and gave me a peck on the cheek. But she didn't. In fact she didn't even look. She didn't even try not to look. She just didn't. Nobody could act that well. No-one could pretend to be as totally and utterly uninterested as Sylvia was right then. She was wearing tracksuit pants. They stuck to her sweaty bum. As she walked towards the dunny she reached around absently and with her thumb and forefinger separated synthetic fibre from the skin of her arse. She wasn't faking it. It is clear to me now that she really *really* didn't give a shit. A little confronting. I must admit that with the relief came a little hurt pride.

I realise now that I was kind of looking forward to the delicious shared secret and the naughtiness of the hidden sin. This was part of the attraction with Mary and Faith. For them as well as me. But I wonder what was going through Sylvia's mind that night. It is almost impossible for me to imagine that actually nothing much was going through her mind. It was really just a physical impulse satisfied. I don't judge her for it. I am hardly one to judge anybody. I'm only now really beginning to see that about myself.

My pride may have been dented but I still had the mental reserves to avoid doing the washing up. I walked purposefully back to my tent as if I had left something important in there, leaving the greasy dishes to the others. I pulled the flap closed and sat in the strange filtered light on my sleeping bag. I drew my knees up to my chest and hugged my shins. I thought it all over and experienced that beautiful sense of relief again. I made my decision: this is the last time that they will make me feel guilt like that. I'd had fun and so had she. We didn't hurt anybody. We brought pleasure to each other. And besides, I knew that in twenty-four hours I was out of there. I lay back on the hard ground under my sleeping bag and waited to be caught.

* * *

On the day I got back to Sydney I spent two hours on the web searching the job vacancies. There was no point looking for a new place until I knew I had a job so I sent my résumé to a couple of clinics looking for counsellors, then caught the bus to The Mission where I spent the afternoon discussing herpes with two madams full of biologically explicit questions. The conversation was a real mood-lifter. In the evening, I locked up The Mission and headed home. There's never much going on in Kings Cross on a Monday night so there was no point hanging around. Soon after dark I found myself back in my quiet home, alone with the ghosts of old lovers. Basically, I had fucked myself to a standstill. Quite an achievement for a preacher in a fundamentalist Christian church. I had spent the last few years healing gall stones on a Sunday and banging like a biscuit tray Monday through Saturday. Sometimes, in fact, on the Sunday as well. I started to feel bad about myself. I wallowed through the evening, forcing over-cooked chops and lumpy mashed potato down my gullet. It was like sawdust on my tongue. Poor Mary. Poor Faith. What a mess I seemed to have made of it. And poor Angela. What a wound I had dealt her! To demonstrate for a woman that love is not always enough! To ruin the fairy tale. Of all my crimes, that was the worst. Mea culpa. Mea culpa. Mea maxima culpa.

And then I compounded it all by sleeping with Sylvia at the Church Retreat. What a piece of work was I. In my quiet lounge room, my chop-smeared plate on my lap, I was tempted to punish myself again. For years now I had not had far to go, never more than a cringe from shame. I worked through the litany of my wrongs against women: Mary, Faith, Angela, Grace, Sylvia. I emotionally flagellated myself for a good hour, through the washing up and into dessert, and then I turned in for the night. Empty bed. Over-full heart.

* * *

This is how it ended:

Gregory telephoned me the Wednesday after the Church Retreat and when I answered he stated tersely that he wanted to see me in his office. Immediately. When I asked why, he told me that a serious allegation had been made against me. He paused for effect and clarified with 'of a *sexual* nature'. He sounded sincerely pissed off so I asked no further questions. I told him I would be there in an hour. I put down the receiver with a calmness that surprised me, collected my keys and strolled outside into glorious sunshine feeling overwhelmed by a sense of weightlessness, a wonderful floating sensation, of liberation. I realised that I *really* could not have cared less what Gregory had to say. On the bus out to the church I thought over the possibilities. Not Mary. Not Faith. They would never have betrayed me. Angela was a possibility but unlikely. She had her reasons to be angry but she was never spiteful. If anything, I think she may even have felt sorry for me. There was Grace of the one-night-stand but she didn't even know my name. So that left Sylvia. Cool as a cucumber, legs akimbo, precocious Sylvia. It all made sense and I could forgive her for it. So young. Poor girl.

So that was my state of mind when I entered Gregory's office an hour later. He gave me a look that said 'the jig is up', but he said nothing, gestured to the chair and looked at me sternly as he circled the desk to sit opposite me. Strangely, I felt like laughing out loud. For the first time in years it occurred to me that I could have just gotten up and walked out of there. There was nothing holding me to that place any more, but I stuck around because there was something that Gregory wanted to get off his chest. I would let him do it. It would all be part of the healing process. He took a deep breath and broke the silence with, 'A very serious allegation has been made against you.' I didn't say anything immediately because I was unsure whether Gregory had more to say. There was quite a long pause as I ordered my own thoughts and formulated an answer that I hoped would give the impression that Gregory seemed to be after. Contrition and shame. Gregory was just opening his mouth to speak again when I interrupted with, 'Yeah. I rooted her.'

The change in Gregory's expression was swift and radical. He transformed from castigating father to shocked five year old in a microsecond. His eyebrows arced to his hairline. He couldn't have looked more surprised if I'd pulled out a gun and shot out the light fittings. 'What? You *what?!*' he exclaimed. Then trying to make sense of things he shook his head and gasped, 'Who?' 'Sylvia,' I replied, nodding encouragingly, as if to say 'yep, you got me.' Gregory looked confused. 'Who in God's name is Sylvia?' he asked in bewilderment. I didn't answer. It began to dawn on me: Oh shit, I've fucked up. We were both just beginning to work that out. I had *really* fucked up. I tried to think quickly on my feet.

'Nobody,' I said like a genius. But I saw the penny drop. 'Sylvia! Sylvia, youth group Sylvia!' cried Gregory. I nodded sheepishly. Gregory shook his head, speechless. He looked very upset. I even felt a bit sorry for him, like I had let him down. I was tempted to walk around the desk and comfort him but he was building up to angry. My mouth went dry, my face burned and then suddenly that other sense again. A sense of relief, liberty, surrender. I recalled that I didn't even *have* to be there. He had no power over me! I knew good from bad and guilt from redemption. I could be my *own* judge. I didn't need his smug condescension. So, fuck him.

I stood to leave and found myself looking down on Gregory who looked back up at me with confusion written all over his face. I shrugged. 'Get out,' he snapped at me. I turned and walked out the door. I got two steps into the corridor when a thought struck me. I turned and walked back into Gregory's office. He was already reaching for the telephone but I had to know. I asked him a little shyly what the allegation made against me was. He took a moment to register the question then answered me in a cold angry voice. 'Donna says that you were perving at her sister.' He put the phone down, looking tired. Even he must have appreciated the banality of her thinking. 'She has reported you for lustful thoughts.'

* * *

Poor Sylvia. I don't think I'll be getting a Christmas card from *her* this year. I had just enough time to feel sorry for her before things really started getting out of hand. First I was evicted from my home. I got the news by text message sent from Gregory's phone. About fifteen minutes later he remembered that he still employed me. A second text message saw me sacked. I packed my few belongings into a couple of suitcases and checked into a hotel for a few days while I got my thoughts together. I just needed to land myself a job and I could put the whole sorry affair behind me. I was far from upset. I actually felt enormous relief, like an escapee, a survivor. The future appeared bright, a life without lies and obfuscations. On my first Sunday morning I slept in. A Sunday morning dedicated to sleep! I could hardly contain my excitement. I rolled out of bed and strolled downstairs after a quick shower. I headed for my favourite café on King Street, buying the weekend newspaper on the way. I found myself a table outside in the sun. I ordered a coffee and the eggs benedict and leant back in my chair thinking, 'This is the life!' I reached for the paper, opened its crisp pages, and read the front page headline: Preacher Caught in Teen Sex Scandal. I felt my bowels shift. My heart thumped in my chest. Holy Christ Al-fucking-mighty! There I was. Me. A photo taken a few years ago at a youth group picnic surrounded by teenaged girls. I scrutinised the picture. Christ, even *I* thought I looked like a pervert. Smiling wanly at the camera, looking every inch the sleaze, an arm around a young girl's shoulders. I read the article with mounting horror. An unnamed source, whose language was uncannily similar to Donna's, reported that I had abused my position to exploit young girls in the Ministry of Christ. It was the word 'girl' that did me such damage. It called to mind a thirteen year old, not the precocious nineteen-year-old Sylvia with the dexterous oral cavity and outdoors fetish. There were dark hints about my familiarity with prostitutes and drug dealers and pimps. I was a fraud and a hypocrite. The last two charges I took on the chin.

Temples pounding and mind whirring, I suddenly remembered where I was. I looked around the café anxiously. No-one seemed to be paying me any attention. Oh thank fuck. All those lucky people just living their lives! I was filled with a sudden envy. I would have changed places with any one of them right then and there (well, not the fat one). I rose from my table, folded the paper under my arm and walked like a robot out onto the street. I began looking now for sanctuary. I high-tailed it for the hotel imagining a hundred eyes on my back and when I got there I headed straight to my room. The corridor outside was empty but for one man a couple of doors up. He was feeling in his pockets for his wallet and I ignored him, but as I swiped my key card and pushed on the door I suddenly became aware that the man had moved quickly to my side. I turned to see him thrust his foot in the door. A camera-man and sound-man had appeared from nowhere. The first man began demanding, 'What have you got to say for yourself? How many girls did you abuse?' I pushed him away but he wouldn't be deterred. I tried to get inside but he stayed with me, dragging the other two men with him. I asked him to leave. I threatened him with trespass charges. I begged him to leave. But he just stood there behind the camera with a self-satisfied smirk. He knew this footage was gold. I knew that the next day my pleading, threatening, anguished, frightened, angry face would be all over the television, and in the background the journalist firing loaded questions at me with that hint of smug arrogance in his voice, and suddenly I felt the enormous weight of six years of being judged crushing down on me, so I did the only rational thing. I took two quick steps towards the journalist and with all my strength smashed his nose across his face. There was sudden silence. He slumped to his knees without a word as the camera-man swung around to get the shot. He was actually laughing. The sound-man looked well pleased with the situation too. I suspect that they didn't like this supercilious bastard any more than I did. And then, just like that, I left the room, walked down the corridor to the stairwell, and ran for my frickin' life.

It went on like that for days. Camera-men staking out my hotel, shock jocks damning me from their pulpits, preachers damning me from theirs, headlines and current affairs programs. I heard them, read them, watched them and didn't even recognise the person that they were talking about. Yet it was me. I had nowhere to go. People pointed at me on the street. No chance of getting that job now. My money was running out. I had become a pariah. And just when I had completely run out of ideas I got an email from an old friend. Mister Theory. It started with, 'Looks like you could use a place to stay ...' He was right of course, as always.

And Now

HOT AND FLAT and dirty-brown, bugger-all water, and a white-blue sky. The Nullarbor Plain. I am here to tell you, there is a hell of a lot of it. I scoot along a strip of ruler-straight oozy-black bitumen in a car that cost me three hundred dollars. The road and I both frayed at the edges. The car rattling like a tin can. I'm heading west, in the direction of away from. Away from the Cross. Away from the cruel headlines. Away from drugs disappearing up arms and wife bashers and smut. It feels *good* to be a coward. What a relief to be running away! I race along the highway with the window down and feel the clean air in my face. There's nothing out here but a road and a bunch of runted trees. Hardly a human for a hundred kilometres at a stretch. And best of all, no God. Just distilled warm sunlight, clarified and clarifying. I press on the accelerator and keep my eye out for a sign that I am told will read 'Last Petrol for 256km', and an old silver beer-can caravan perched on top of a 30-foot pole. It's the sign for the petrol station that Mister Theory now owns. It is where he has guaranteed me a bed but advised me not to hold my breath for nooky. Unless I like truck drivers.

I see the petrol station from what seems like a hundred miles. It shimmers in the distance as my old rattler struggles down the highway. At the turn-off, I slow and roll into the parking area next to a besser-block building. Old-style bowsers hunch in the shade of a corrugated metal awning. I turn off the engine and step out of the car. A heavy blanket of heat and silence. I hear the squeak of a door and turn to see a man exit the station house in a wheelchair. He's dressed in black and wears a gold chain. It's Mister Theory. A friendly face. And it's all I can do not to kiss him.

It's dim inside the station house and only marginally cooler than outside. Mister Theory explains, 'The light here is so bright it hurts the eyes. I used to get headaches from squinting it out all day. So in here I leave the lights off. To rest my eyes. And the air con just didn't feel right.' Mister Theory looks well, in spite of the wheelchair. There are subjects between us that want to be spoken but which can wait. Life in a wheelchair. Sex scandals. The closest we come to these subjects is a light quip from Mister

Theory. 'Sounds like you've been getting a bit then,' he says with a cheeky smile. I say nothing and he doesn't push it. 'So where do I sleep?' I ask and Mister Theory smiles again. 'You've already seen it,' he replies. He grips the rims of his wheels and rolls outside with me following. We both squint as we exit onto the Nullarbor. Mister Theory gestures with a flick of his head to the caravan on the pole. 'Home sweet home,' he says. I tilt my head back to look up at the old round caravan. It is bright silver and radiates the sun like a mirror. I notice for the first time that a narrow ladder leads up the pole to a hole in its floor. Through the hole, Mister Theory tells me, is a bed, television and bar fridge. I notice for the first time that behind the station house there are four small cabins in a row. 'What's wrong with them?' I ask. 'Nothing,' he says. 'Then why can't I sleep in there?' Mister Theory shakes his head matter-of-factly as he pulls on one wheel to pivot and return to the station house. 'You can't use them,' he calls out as he heads back inside. 'They're for the hookers.'

*   *   *

The women that I've had sex with. Because they wanted to. Because they were feeling sexy. Because they were curious. Because they weren't feeling good about themselves. Because they were drunk. Because they were lonely. Because it was naughty. Because they thought that I was more interesting than I really am. Because they wanted to console me. Because they hadn't worked out how to dump me yet. Because they were bored. Because they were sad. Because they didn't care any more. Because it didn't matter. Because they were aroused by me. Because they didn't want to hurt my feelings. Because it was habit. Because they were getting over someone else. Because they wanted a fuck. Because they were in love.

*   *   *

The trucks run all night. They are a growl in the distance that firms its resolve over a couple of minutes before becoming a

174

brief howl and a receding swish. I lie in my bed at night atop my pole, inside my comfy little caravan, and listen to the night that fills the long gaps between them. Sometimes I watch a snow-hazy television screen. Sometimes I lie in the dark silence sipping a beer, listening to the occasional truck brake and roll into the parking area. Sometimes I hear the driver strike up a conversation with Judy, Danii or Sue, a cabin door close gently, and several minutes of bed-spring squeaking. Mister Theory tells me he's making money hand over fist. He seems well pleased with himself but he's welcome to it. I can't bear that world any more. I leave the girls to the girls. I keep to myself after dark. In the daytime I pump petrol into over-heated tanks and take money from thirsty tourists stocking up on liquids between truck stops. An ascetic life. Plenty of time to wallow. No word from the people that loved me. Nothing from Angela. Nothing from Mary or Faith. No word from Evie or my congregation of Old Testamenters.

At first it makes me angry. I mope around the place feeling alone and let down but Mister Theory is a good tonic. He grows especially assertive when one evening I criticise Angela. 'Leave her alone, Simon,' he says testily. 'She didn't do anything so bad, anything that you haven't done yourself. Stop being a Christian. She loved you, remember.' And the others? The Christians that I taught forgiveness and love? Not a word from them. But Mister Theory explains that for me as well. 'Don't worry about people, they will always let you down,' he tells me. It's hardly uplifting advice. 'So what's that do for me?' I demand. Mister Theory almost looks surprised when he answers. 'You let them down didn't you?'

Over the weeks I begin to lose the tension and the sense of betrayal. I learn to accept my own role in it all. I should have kept it in my trousers, I know. Shoulda. Didn't. I begin to find perspective gazing out over a horizon as flat and sharp as a well-thrown Frisbee. I begin to consider the possibility of redemption. And I wonder sometimes where the sins were. Sin is more complicated than it seems.

But it has to end. Somehow word gets out. I am lying in my bed one evening in my underpants when the trapdoor in the middle of my floor, leading onto the ladder, creaks open and a man's head appears. Before I can do or say anything, a camera flashes and the head disappears, the door slapping shut behind it. The next day a photograph of me appears on the front page of the local rag under the headline: Rogue Sex Preacher Takes up Residence. It's hard to make me out but the confusion on my face and the undies are unmistakable. Two days later, same bed, same trapdoor, I hear a knocking. I'm fully dressed this time when I open it, lean over the hole and gaze down at a woman's face gazing up. She's from a big city tabloid. She'd like to give me a chance to present my side of the story, she lies to me. I let her in, not because I care, but because I couldn't care less. There's only the bed in my caravan so she sits at one end on the edge of it, feet on the floor, while I sit at the other end, back against the bedhead, knees drawn up, facing her. She's in profile for most of the interview, turning from time to time to look penetratingly at me. She is earnest and ardent and has an infallible moral compass. She should be in the Ministry of Christ. Her questions are not questions, they are thinly disguised statements, criticisms, judgements, proceeding from a sense of indignant righteousness. But worst of all they emanate from *certainty*. The woman is around forty years old. Her attitude is inexcusable. She is old enough to have worked out by now that nothing about humans is certain. She launches her interrogation with a sneer.

'How do you respond to those people that say you are evil?'

'I tell them that I am a good man.'

'Good! How can you say 'good'? You took money from good people and gave it to bad people.'

'I did no such thing.'

'You seduced an innocent girl. You supplied drugs to prostitutes.'

'No.'

'Yes.'

'Good men sometimes do evil things. Or things, at least, that aren't exactly good.'

'Are you saying it was the girl's fault?'

'No.'

'Are you a hypocrite?'

'Yes.'

'And a liar?'

'Yes.'

'That's wickedness isn't it?'

'I don't know.'

'You don't know? You were a preacher for six years!'

'I suppose I have come round to thinking that it's all a little more complicated than that.'

'There are rules. You broke some of the fundamental rules of our society.'

'Your rules are very neat.'

'Have you ever had an affair?'

'Yes.'

'While you were a preacher?'

'Yes.'

'Who with?'

'I choose not to answer that. That's none of your business.'

'Aren't you ashamed?'

'No.'

'No! How can you not be ashamed?'

'Because I loved them.'

'So you are an adulterer and a fornicator.'

'Yes.'

'And proud of it!'

'Not proud. Just not ashamed. Proud of *them*. The women. They were all lovely. They were strong and kind. I loved them.'

'Aren't these things sins?'

'Against whom?'

'God.'

'I don't believe in God.'

'The husbands?'

'Yes. Although they are unaware of the hurt I did them and are still with their wives, maybe even *because* of me. Besides, the men too were sinning against their wives, if meanness is a sin.'

177

'The women?'

'No. I never sinned against the women.'

'How can you see so little *wrong* with what you have done?'

'You over-simplify us.'

'Who is 'us'? You think you are so complex?'

'Not me. Not them. Humans. You over-simplify humans. Is there a bigger sin?'

'Some people might say "how dare you?" '

'*You* would say "how dare you".'

'Maybe. Yes. I would.'

'You are wrong. You degrade. You are like the people I used to preach to. Labelling because it's easier than empathising and understanding. Condemning because it's easier and more entertaining than to live your own life and let others live theirs. Prostitutes: wicked. Fornicators: evil. Gays: horrid. Lonely people desiring the company of others: sinners. If your own life were richer then you would show less interest in my mundane one.'

'So you have done nothing wrong.'

'I didn't say that. It's just that I haven't sinned.'

'So what *wrong* have you done?'

'I told sick people that they could be cured by a god. I told needy people that there is a heaven.'

'What's wrong with that? You've given them hope.'

'I've given them no such thing.'

'More?'

'Sylvia. Because my motivations were wrong, and because she was young and still learning.'

'That is disgusting.'

'About life, I mean. Not sex. Sex has nothing to do with it. I worry that I have tainted her thinking now. I worry that she will approach her next relationship with timidity and fear.'

'And more?'

'A woman that I had a relationship with. I made her feel like she had something to be ashamed of.'

'What?'

'Her sex. Her sexiness.'

'Others?'

'Two old ladies who needed me.'

'Any other wrongs? The married women?'

'No.'

'No? You keep saying no.'

'Because I loved them.'

'That cures everything does it?'

'No. But it explains it.'

* * *

The next morning two things arrive for me. The first, a copy of the tabloid. I flick the front page over and there I am on Page 3. A photo of me, staring down the camera, and the headline: Desert Philosopher Preaches Poison. The second, an envelope with a British stamp on it. I open it and a small photograph slips out. It is of a pudgy infant with a gummy grin. On the back of the picture, in Faith's handwriting, the words 'With love. And thank you.'

* * *

The newspaper article has a strange effect. Overnight, people begin visiting me in my pole-top caravan. All day every day, dusty cars pull into the service station and weary drivers ease themselves out. Sweat circles across their shoulders, they pump petrol into their cars, eyeing my caravan with interest before strolling into the building to pay Mister Theory. Exiting a few minutes later, licking ice creams or sipping Cokes, they walk across to my ladder and start climbing. They behave as if I have been expecting them, like we know each other from many years ago and can dispense with the preliminaries, the courtesies. Sitting on my bed I do what I have trained to do over the last few years. I listen while they talk. I learn that the world is full of confusion and that most people really do try their best. They don't want to cause pain. And they don't want to feel it. They are looking for answers in a million different ways. Through counselling, at pilates, book clubs, church. There are middle-aged men who worry themselves sick because the infants that they once cuddled and nurtured are now rebellious adolescents who throw tantrums and swear them out of their lives. There are women who want to love but who fear for their husbands who have lost their warmth and who may love them no more. There are teens buzzing with hormones who lash out in anger, crumple in sorrow. There are people that want guidance and get nothing from a preacher who says 'Do it my way because I have God on my side.' There are people that need to be told that they are humans and therefore have the right to make errors. In the end, there are just people.

So in my little caravan, on the top of a pole, I invent a new religion. It is a soothing and understanding one. It is godless but not without its strictures: do not hurt other people, but if you do, don't be too hard on yourself. You're not going to hell, because there is no hell. If you have erred, you can maybe make it right on earth. Work to that. Work hard. In my new religion we accept that the world is an arse. Sometimes bad things happen to good people. Sometimes good things happen to bad ones. There is no grand cosmic equaliser. That's not how it works. So ignore the scaredy-cats. Live your life in the manner that brings you pleasure while not bringing pain to others. Follow a religion that says, have a go, don't be afraid, roll with the punches. Snub those that judge you from their cosseted comfy lives. If you make a mistake and are truly regretful, you are not a sinner. You are a person.

I'd like to think that people leave my little caravan, perched on the top of its pole, feeling better. Certainly, I've had a great many approach me with tears in their eyes and leave with a warm hug for me and a smile. I take no money for my religion. If I did that, it would be tainted. It would not, in fact, be a religion. But Mister Theory pays me to pump petrol and clean the cabins and stock the shelves. It's a good life. I'll go back to the city one day. Maybe even soon. I'll go back to the Cross and help the working girls like I did before, because although it's hard, it is also the right thing to do. A life spent not helping is not really much of a life actually. But I won't go back there yet. I'll stay here for a little

longer, eye on that crisp horizon, head rushing with the purity of the desert breeze.

* * *

A small package arrives in the post one day. I open it and a chocolate bar falls out. Inside is a card from Evie. It says 'Hi Preacher. You are very *very* naughty. But nice, I suppose. I'm well. Love, E'.

* * *

A few days later, another letter. This one from Patti. She tells me that she misses me, that I'm a duffer, but to err is human. She tells me also that she has found a new church, given up on the Ministry of Christ, who are all a bunch of miserable buggers. Am I eating properly? And she tells me that Pru's will makes for interesting reading, by the way. If I'm ever keen to start a new mission in the Cross, that is.

* * *

One evening, lying on my bed, I hear movement at the foot of the caravan's pole. I open my trapdoor and look down in the gloom. I can see a woman below, preparing to ascend the ladder. She has dark hair and wears jeans and a light jumper. She looks up at the trapdoor, readies herself, and begins to climb. A truck roars past on the highway. It takes whole seconds for the three trailers to roll by, a blur of lights and sound. The woman pauses halfway up to watch it, then as the sound and lights recede she begins climbing again. I watch her with some interest. Her movements are familiar to me but I can't make out her features until she is just a couple of rungs from me. The light in her eyes! My heart lifts. I extend my hand and feel it taken. I help Mary into my caravan. I lower the trapdoor and do away with the world. Without speaking she falls into my arms. I hold her warm body against my own, feeling its inner power, the beating of her pulse, the rise and fall of her breathing, the touch of her hands. My God I have missed these things. Mary and her wonderful body, the spirit pulsing within it, her affection and love. Her life. I draw her to me, into me, gasping her into my lungs. She buries her face into the hollow of my throat. I feel her soft lips on my skin, her nose squished against my Adam's apple. Finally, we separate, reluctantly, and face each other. She takes a breath to speak. Her voice is calm but very sad. 'My daughter has died, Simon. She is dead.' I'm holding Mary's hand. She takes a deep breath. 'She was such a good girl,' she gasps, blinking tears. We sit on the bed speechless, reaching out our hands, feeling each other, touching shoulders, faces, knees. If I feel her, she must be real. I put my arms around Mary's upper body, a tight circle that I hope she will never escape. She submits to the embrace, turned against my body, both her hands in my lap. She does not cry, brave Mary. A half minute passes, my palms resting on the blades of her shoulders. 'And Donald?' I ask. She answers softly, 'I've left him.' Mary looks into my face and asks, 'Can I stay with you for a while?' 'Yes,' I answer. 'For as long as you like.' She takes my right hand and kisses it. I want to hug her into my pores, absorb her. Then opening her legs slightly Mary presses my hand to her groin. It is a gesture of love and intense purity. Sinless.